THE LAST STOP

THE
LAST STOP

KIRT J BOYD

For Cinder and Sully, a.k.a Cinder Block and Hoss

"We are not one of those places where carpet is an amenity."
—*Mary Stuart Riley*

Welcome Home!

No old fogies allowed! We at The Mary Stuart Riley Home for People of Advanced Years (affectionately nicknamed The Last Stop) believe that you are only as old as you feel, and it is our sole mission to make you feel great. We encourage a youthfulness of mind, body and spirit not found in other homes. We are not a "Facility," and while we like Nursing as a profession, you will not catch the word mucking up our signs or our reputation. We are a Home, in the best sense of the word.

We do not advocate surrendering to the effects of old age and slipping peacefully into the hereafter, and if you try, your fellow white-hairs will pull you back by your ankles, all the while chanting something indecipherable but which can only mean LIFE. No one ever dies at The Last Stop; they just decide to move on.

Through our three-pronged activities programs and social events, you will not have the time or the desire to sit idle while the best years of your life pass you by. To keep your mind sharp and inspired, we have speakers on a wide variety of subjects every Thursday night; we have a Fitness Center filled with the latest and greatest equipment for all your exercise and aquatic needs; we have a game room any twelve-year old boy would be at home in; we have acres of walking trails, and weekly excursions where the residents choose the destinations. And we have our 165lb mascot, Holy Moses: the only canine on earth that likes cherry twizzlers, runs towards fireworks, and can be rented out as a sleeping companion.

And that's just the beginning. So come celebrate the glory of life with people who know that age is a state of mind, and where The Reaper carries a foam bat and steals strawberries from the buffet table.

From the Archives
The Last Stop Bulletin

The Weather Front

Well, for those of you fond of hurricanes, you're in luck. While we are over a thousand miles from the nearest ocean, you would never know it to look out the window. If we had palm trees, they would be beating themselves to death, and if we had committed weather people like they do on the Today Show, who tether themselves and blow out their voices shouting at us, at least then we would have something entertaining to watch. But, alas, we have neither, so we'll just have to use our imaginations. Yesterday, we described the rain as, "coming down in buckets," and the day before that, we described it as a "ferocious downpour." Today the word that comes to mind is Deluge from the Latin word Diluvium, to wash away. It has a certain ring to it.

Upcoming Events

Friday's movie will be *Terms of Endearment*, back by popular demand. It has been six months, and we all know how beneficial uncontrollable sobbing can be to overall health. Ms. Theron, we only ask that you keep your adoration for Jack to yourself or you will be asked to sit in back. We all love him, but shouting, "Come to momma!" every time he makes an appearance is both inappropriate and inconsiderate to the other moviegoers, who, believe it or not, actually like the movie for the story.

Also, don't forget that we will be starting our Cary Grant film festival next Friday evening with a six o'clock showing of *His Girl Friday*. Sometimes we all need Cary Grant, even you Robert.

YOU OUGHT TO KNOW

Beauty Inc. will be closed through Wednesday for emergency hairdryer replacement after Ms. Verney's hair caught on fire. We are happy to report that she is doing well and should be out of the hospital in a couple of weeks. She doesn't want visitors because she has no hair at present; we understand completely.

Because of the traumatic nature of the incident, we would like to take this opportunity to reassure you of the safety of Beauty Inc. There is no need for panic. And, for the record, yes her head was on fire, but the flames were not licking the ceiling. This is the first incident in nearly two years, and the first since we started using the safety scissors. Some of you have suggested canceling this week's book club discussion of *Fahrenheit 451* out of respect for Ms. Verney, but she wishes you to push on without her. What a trooper. There is a Get Well card in Reception if you would like to sign it. We would also like to thank Ms. Hancock who offered to make Ms. Verney a wig out of her own hair. That will be unnecessary, but thank you none the less.

THE HOT SEAT

Please take a seat Mr. Udall and make yourself comfy. When you told Chef Amato that the eggs were runny and made you gag, he went crazy and started throwing things at the new kid, Nathan, who has already had it up to here. Amato doesn't do criticism, and such outbursts put us all at risk. And speaking of Nathan, he is coming up on his one week anniversary, which is exactly three day longer than the previous six cooks so we're thinking about throwing him some kind of a party.

THE SUGGESTION BOX

You have spoken and we have listened. Due to the overwhelming number of complaints, the choir will be wrapping up their rehearsal by eight o'clock. It's not the volume so much as it is the variety of keys that are being "sung" simultaneously. This is not a knock on those of you in the choir. We are confident that you will be good one day, it just hasn't happened yet. Don't worry. You still have six months until Christmas.

Holy Moses!

Mr. Robinson's three year old grandson scoured the web for something that would cure snoring in dogs, but came back with more bad news. It turns out that snoring is particularly hard to curb in Bull Dogs and Mastiffs, and since our boy is of the English Mastiff variety, we are just going to have to deal with it. We know it can be rough going if he picks your door to sleep by, so if anyone knows of a company that sells earplugs in bulk, please let us know. We're sorry, Ms. Thatcher, but we're going to have to turn down your request to let Holy sleep in your bed with you. We wouldn't want you to get pinned like Mr. Patterson did. Holy might also decide he doesn't want to share your bed with you, and then what would you do?

ORIENTATION

He isn't dead, if that's what you're wondering. It's just Robert. Just be glad his robe is tied or you'd be seeing things you wish you hadn't. Every morning at six o'clock sharp, he comes out here and eats raisins until visitors start showing up, then he flops over and plays dead. And when some cute blonde comes rushing over to revive him, he grabs her and starts kissing her with his dirty little mouth…Just between you and me, I felt like smothering the little worm, but the training manual strictly prohibits it.

He's gotten really good at it. He says he can slow his heart rate way down, which is dangerous considering his age. He even starred on Broadway back in the fifties. He played Torvald Helmer in *A Doll House* by someone named Ibsen. You know how I know? Because every time he comes through Reception he says, "Is that my little lark twittering over there? Is that my squirrel rummaging around?" which I guess was one of his lines. I keep telling him my name is Beverly, but he keeps calling me his little lark, whatever that is. Don't let him corner you or he'll tell you the whole story. You might even end up being the squirrel and you wouldn't want that.

The porch swing broke last year and was out of service for a week, so Robert had to do the whole routine on one of those metal folding chairs. He walked funny for a couple weeks after that. He told me that he once fell asleep in the overhead rack on a flight to Tampa Bay, but he might have been pulling my leg.

He does wear underwear now, thank god. All the nurses pitched in and bought him thirty-two pairs of boxer shorts after being surprised one too many times. If you could somehow bottle that man's libido you'd be one rich duck.

Anyway, he'll be out here until Byron shows up to do his morning calisthenics. Robert is scared to death of him. Byron was in the 1956 Olympic Games in Melbourne, and came close to winning a bronze medal in both the long jump and the pole vault. He won't let anyone forget it, either. He says he's got his eye on the 2016 Games. We took the pole vault away from him a few years ago because he kept coming up short and landing in the rosebushes. He still practices the long jump over by the Fitness Center, though, and he uses the hedges over there as hurdles.

Here comes Holy Moses. No, it's all right. I know it's scary when he circles you like that, but he's just checking you out. He'll respond to Holy or Moses, or just about anything else if he thinks you have access to cheese. We're supposed to quit feeding him junk food on account of his weight, but if you don't give him what he wants he usually takes it anyway so why go through all the trouble?

When he swats at you with his paw, you're supposed to pet him. You don't want him to put a little red check next to your name. Go for a hug next time. He loves hugs. That'll probably make up for it.

Sorry, he got a little on you. He's a crazy drooler. Most of the residents carry a towel or something just in case. He's a crazy pooper, too. That's why there are poop bag stations all over the place. Everyone helps clean up after him because it's more than one person can handle. I think he poops when he's bored. Sometimes I poop when I'm bored, too…just kidding! I just wanted to see the look on your face.

Anyway, Holy drives Harry—that's our maintenance man—crazy because sometimes he squeezes back behind bushes to do his business so Harry has to get on his hands and knees and go hunting for it. Or sometimes he poops while he walks so Harry has to follow him around. Don't worry, he only does that to Harry; it's their little game.

When Harry's really mad he tells Holy the story of *Old Yeller*. Isn't that terrible? Like Harry would ever shoot him, even if he did have rabies. He'd probably just build a special rabies-proof room for Holy to live in where he couldn't hurt anyone. Harry actually found Holy wandering down by the river six years ago. No collar or anything. Holy was chasing bugs and tripped over his feet and fell in the river and was swept away by the current. Harry ran half a mile along the path until Holy finally got hung up on a downed tree and he was able to swim out and rescue him.

Harry always tells the story at the Christmas party after he's had a few drinks to loosen him up. Anyway, when Harry got out to him, the first thing he said was, "Holy Moses!" and the name stuck. The first thing Mary Stuart said when Harry brought him here was, "Holy Shit," but it didn't have quite the same ring to it. Holy was just a baby then, but he already weighed forty pounds, and his feet were huge. You ever see a little kid wearing his dad's boots? That's what he looked like.

Don't worry, he'll be back. He's figured out that new people give him more treats, either because he's so darned cute or so darned scary depending on your perspective.

Okay, I wasn't going to tell you this, but you'll probably hear about it so…We used to have fish right over there by the window but I thought they were plastic and now they're in fish heaven. I know, I know, plastic fish can't swim. Whatever. I also thought the plants were real and I watered them like crazy. Boy was I mixed up. So, anyway, I didn't feed them, not once, and they started eating each other and charging the glass. How was I supposed to know? They were way over there and who checks on plastic fish? Anyway, I kept hearing this knocking sound and I couldn't figure out where it was coming from, and then…

Once they taste flesh they never go back to regular fish food. There were only two of them left and I couldn't stand watching them fight all the time so I said a little prayer and flushed them down the toilet. Does that make me a bad person? I don't know. I think about them a lot. I can still see their angry, little faces glaring up at me going round and round… So, anyway, if you want to see fish, you'll have to go down to the river with a net.

Now it's where we keep The Suggestion Box. You know what the first suggestion was? That we don't get any more fish—smart alecks. Anyway, the chin-wags go through the suggestions and report on them in The Last Stop Bulletin, our resident newsletter. Yes, they like to be called the chin-wags. They even have matching t-shirts that say, "The Mighty Chin-wags," which they think is hysterical.

From the Archives
The Last Stop Bulletin

The Weather Front

We live in Colorado and apparently Mother Nature wants to remind us of the fact. The shorts, sun dresses, flip-flops and tank tops you had anticipated wearing when the rain finally stopped can be repacked into your summer bins and thrown back in the attic. Instead of stopping the rain, Mother Nature apparently thinks it would be funny to turn it to snow sometime around the noon hour. Yesterday's high of fifty-three will feel downright balmy compared to today's forecasted high of thirty-seven. It is the last week of May, right, or did our watches stop? Anyway, we did hear some mention of high pressure building, but we'll believe it when we see it. Don't break out the sleds and snowshoes; the snow is not actually going to stick.

Upcoming Events

There is still time to sign up for the new Yoga for Life class starting Monday morning. I guess we should tell you that there is a new Yoga class starting Monday morning, since it's just been pointed out that we neglected to do so. So, guess what? There is a new Yoga class starting Monday morning. It's a coed class, and Kelly (of course) will be your instructor. The new mats should be in sometime today, so come get your sweat on. Kelly promises not to work you too hard the first day, but that's what she always says.

YOU OUGHT TO KNOW

Mary Stuart is not feeling well today; not surprising considering the weather, and she will not be making her normal rounds. Mary hasn't been sick since the summer of 1977, so the bug that bit her must be particularly nasty. Because of this, we ask that you don't go up and visit her. If you would like to wish her well, simply take the elevator up to Health Care, and when the door opens, stick your head out and yell whatever you want until the door closes and takes you back down. There is a Get Well card in Reception, but since it's only been a day, we see no sense in using it prematurely.

THE HOT SEAT

See The Suggestion Box

THE SUGGESTION BOX

You have spoken and we have listened, but no, Ms. Theron, it is not appropriate for us to ask Nathan to take his shirt off. That isn't what we had in mind when we started asking for input. Besides, he is much, much too young for you, and while we believe you when you say his arms remind you of smoked hams, we really must ask you to keep the dirty talk to a minimum, at least when you're within shouting distance of the kitchen. Nathan has a lot to contend with already without being molested by a bunch of sex-crazed white-hairs.

HOLY MOSES!

Please, no more peanut butter or onion rings. We have found mountains of Holy hurl all over the building. At 169lbs, he is 19lbs over his ideal weight, so let's try to stick to his regular food except on special occasions. It will be hard for him at first, but it's for his own good. We know he can be demanding at times and he's not above throwing his weight around, but please be strong. Just explain it to him. He's a good listener, and if he doesn't quite understand what you're saying, he will appreciate the effort.

ORIENTATION CONT.

Copies of The Last Stop Bulletin are in a basket down in the Activities Room back by the bulletin board. You can't miss it. It's under the painting of a bunch of old people dancing in a graveyard. The chin-wags picked it out. The Bulletin archives going back to nineteen eighty-eight are kept in the library vault. You have to ask for them special, and you can't take them with you. The chin-wags have this crazy idea that they will one day be collected in book form and become a classic in Assisted Living Literature.

Friday is movie night. I hope you like Cary Grant. You'll see why when you go to the theater. There's a poster from every movie he's ever been in. There's also a framed photograph from *His Girl Friday*, signed by both Cary Grant and Rosalind Russell, which is her prized possession. There used to be a life-sized cardboard cutout of Cary greeting you as you went into the theater, but part of his mouth got torn, making him look like some sort of weird Cary Grant zombie and it gave everyone the creeps, so Mary finally got rid of it.

Sometimes Randy—that's our driver—will take groups to an offsite theater if there's a new release that everyone just can't wait to see, but that doesn't happen very often. We have our own concession stand with everything you could possibly want and our seats are way more comfortable than regular theater seats. We've even got a balcony like the ones back in the fifties. I don't know if it's exactly the same, though, because that was way, way before I was born. Some of the men dress up and work as ushers, too, like they did in the olden days. You've got to see them with their little hats and gloves. Some of the more serious ones even walk around with little flashlights to make sure no one is doing anything inappropriate. Oh, and Holy Moses usually shows up, too, because of the popcorn, so if he's suddenly sitting in the chair next to you, breathing in your hair, don't freak out.

One thing about the Activities Room: stay clear of the dartboard. Most of the guys can't see very well anymore and they make up for it by throwing harder, so watch out…This is the Community Board. As you can see, Harry is our most frequent contributor. "Stay off the grass!" is one of his favorites during the summer months. People cutting across the lawn to the Fitness Center wore a footpath in Harry's Kentucky Blue Grass and he spent three days digging it up and replacing it. That was seven summers ago. He still hasn't let it go. Beginning in April, he starts posting reminders. So if you don't want him to chase you around with a rake, use the stone path.

He will also use the board for upcoming projects; painting, for instance, or floor waxing. Don't worry too much about it, though: He uses so many signs and red tape, that it's not physically possible to breech the "danger zone."

Also, he's super crazy about trash, and not in a good way. Every morning he walks the grounds looking for "contaminants." He can spot a cigarette butt from three hundred yards. You can always tell when it happens because he starts blinking really fast and then he usually throws his bucket. We keep telling him that most of the trash comes from visitors, but he holds us all responsible for not stressing his "Pack it out" policy strongly enough.

I don't know if you smoke, but if you do it's going to get bumpy. Kelly is our fitness instructor and if she finds out you're a smoker, she'll start slipping shock photos under your door. Things like giant tumors and lungs that look like grilled eggplant…

I hate to leave you with that image, but I have to get back to my desk. If you need anything, you know where to find me. The restaurant is down the hall and around the corner if you're hungry. It used to be called The Last Supper, but our chef, Amato, is sketchy enough without encouraging him, so now it's nameless. Everything else you need to know is in your handbook. Or you can just ask someone. Everyone is very chatty around here, as you'll soon find out.

CASSANDRA

Is that a painting of Mozart? I love Mozart. I know, I know, I don't look like someone who likes Mozart, but I was listening to some G minor thing this morning as part of a new program about enriching your life through music and I think I'm in love. It's just too bad he's dead.

Let me see your arm…I just want to get your blood pressure real quick. Anyway, I was skeptical at first. Music is music, right? You either like it or you don't. There's nothing…what's the word she used?… Transcending, there's nothing transcending about it. That's what I thought, anyway. Now I'm not so sure. They turned off the lights and had us put headphones on and…I don't know if I was transformed but I was trans-something-ed.

Open your mouth and say ahhhh…We like to do checkups in resident's rooms. It's more comfortable this way. If you were wondering, that's all. Don't worry, it's only once a month, so it's not like I'll come barging in every other day. All right, lay back…So the instructor told us stories about people who had never heard classical music before being introduced to Mozart and actually breaking down; grown men with tattoos and everything. And now there are studies that show that playing Mozart to babies in the womb actually might make them smarter. It's called the Mozart-Effect. Anyway, it was all news to me. No one in the neighborhood I grew up in listened to classical music, that's for sure. And the idiot I lived with for the last six years wouldn't know a violin if it was stuck up his…

Stand up. Let's get a look in your ears…So my question is: what else have I missed out on? If I went twenty-seven years without knowing that Mozart even existed, what else is there I don't know about? What about Poetry? Or History. Or Art, for crying out loud. If you want to talk about Art, you'd be better off talking to that fork. It's driving me crazy. I don't even know where to begin.

Okay, that's it. And I have bad news for you: as far as I can tell you are perfectly healthy. We're big believers in fighting aging through diet and exercise. We don't like medication unless absolutely necessary. We do use them, of course, but the best treatment is not having anything to treat, right?

Now if we can just get you to smile a bit more you'll be all set. I know, it's not quite like home, but you're going to love it here, trust me, everybody does. The place I worked before here, Green Willows, now that place was awful. It was small and claustrophobic and the lighting was bad and it smelled weird all the time. The residents were miserable; the staff was miserable. The halls got so crowded at certain times of the day that it was like a high school between classes. And did I mention that it smelled weird?

I thought all assisted living places were like that until a friend of my mother's told me about this place and I came down and interviewed with Mary Stuart. All I had to go on was the brochure, which looked great, of course, but they all do. If all you knew about Green Willows was from the brochure, you'd think the residents divided their time between hugging loved ones and singing around the piano. They didn't even have a piano. They rented one for the day. I think they rented the old people, too, because I didn't recognize any of them. But when I showed up here and met Mary I realized that the brochure didn't even do it justice.

Mary didn't interview me. All we did was walk around and talk. She didn't even look at my application. After a half hour or so, she offered me the job. Just like that. I was confused because we hadn't talked much about my experience at all. I'll never forget it. She said: "I'm not interested in people who are looking for a job. I want people who make a difference. That is what I require. The rest can be learned."

That was a year ago yesterday. That's when I changed everything. I left my boyfriend—well, he didn't really have a choice because he went to jail, but I would have left him anyway. And since then...sorry, I'll stop. You don't need my life story. I'm not crazy, I swear.

15

So, anyway, I'm your Care Provider. Your buzzer over there goes directly to me, so if you need anything don't hesitate. I used to hate that buzzer when I first started. Robert—the guy you saw on the porch swing—used to buzz me fifty times a day. "Ms. Cassandra, can I get a glass of water?" As if he's incapable of getting his own water. "Ms. Cassandra, can you help me find my other green sock." He loves that one. After you spend fifteen minutes searching, you realize he doesn't own a pair of green socks and never has, and you want to drown him in the tub.

ASTER

L isten to this and tell me what you think. I've been working on it all morning. A friend of mine, Charlie Bates, whom I went to school with eight hundred years ago, and who had the misfortune of fathering two children who grew up to be raving ingrates, is currently living out a life sentence at a little house of horrors called Sunny Forest out east of Byers. The man is six months younger than I am, and yet while I'm out here drinking lemonade and working on my suntan, he's spending most of his time in bed waiting to die. This, you understand, mustn't continue. He used to be the symbol of health and verve, having had a brief but spectacular track and field career in high school, and now he's sipping his food through a straw and plotting some environment-inspired slow death. So I decided to whip up a brief letter stating my concerns on Charlie's behalf, in hopes of improving conditions. If this fails, you might have to help me smuggle him out in a potato sack. I may have overstated some things, taking liberties here in there with details, but I think I've captured the gist of it.

Dear Sirs and Madams:

Finding myself in no mood for formalities, I'll get right to the point. After much deliberation, I have come to the conclusion that the members of your staff have missed their calling when they decided to care for the elderly. While the staff socialize and draw straws to determine who will do the less desirable duties, the residents are left to fend for themselves. Something as simple as changing the bedding must be pleaded for and made to seem a matter of life and death before any action is taken. And then the task is carried out in such a way that the person making the request is made to feel that they are actively jamming a sewing needle into the eyeball of the unfortunate lazy-ass making the bed. I don't normally resort to such language, but a grape is grape is a grape, and so is a lazy-ass.

And while we are on the subject, the food, if one can call it that, is not fit for human consumption. I have twice found fingernail clippings in what passes for chicken noodle soup, and Ms. Betty choked for several minutes on what appeared to be yarn in her gravy. I decided against telling her that it looked remarkably similar to the yarn I had observed Socks, the eye-weeping, three-legged kitty yakking up that morning. However, it was impossible to make a positive identification because the lighting throughout the facility has one rummaging around for razor blades.

I find myself ranting now, but I can't help pointing out that the noise level makes normal conversation, let alone sleep, impossible. It would seem to me that after hearing for the seven hundredth time the word, "Water!" shouted in that horrible monotone the staff would figure out that Ms. Henley is thirsty.

In closing, the staff is rude, and, in my estimation, incompetent—not to be confused with incontinent, though I wouldn't doubt if they were that, too—and should be disposed of immediately.

I implore you to tackle these issues at once, or I will be forced to take to the streets and shout out my concerns.

P.S. Geraldo Rivera is just a phone call away.

What do you think? The details are mostly fabricated, but in a place like that they are all too possible. Too strong, do you think? Charlie would be incapable of writing this. Charlie's response to life's atrocities has always been to shuffle his feet and then meet it head on with an apologetic smile. Timid is a cruel word, as is meek, but I'm afraid he has been stricken by both conditions.

Ms. Fisher

Dearest Laverne:

Sorry, I would have given word sooner, but I've been laid up in the hospital for close to a week. That's where I am as I write this: lying in bed in this scratchy gown they gave me, trying to find something to pry open the window so I can throw myself out into the parking lot.

No, I'm not dying, as far as I know. You wouldn't think that would be something they'd keep from you. I came in for a broken tooth, and they figured while they had me here they might as well Find Something because they're in the business of Finding Something. It was ridiculous. They wheeled me into this experimental chamber, and one team started sticking me with needles so they could inspect my blood, and another team began poking and prodding me, looking for lumps and discolorations, which, incidentally, there were a lot of because I bruise easily. It's all foolishness. Nothing in the world wrong with me other than the fact that I look ridiculous and I whistle when I speak. The only thing that concerns me is that I might not be able to eat my Gala apples off the core anymore.

So I'm sure you're wondering what happened to my tooth. Well, if you can believe it, I knocked it out on the side of the tub after slipping on a loofah that Jenny bought me for Mother's Day. It was no accident. Jenny knows I don't have rails in the shower to hang onto. You know she watched me put the damned thing in the bathroom because she was afraid I was going to throw it in storage with all the other crap I've gotten over the years. Anyway, I'm not used to having things cluttering up my tub and I forgot it was there and, well, WHAM!

Have you ever gone down in the tub? I'd always thought that that outrageous statistic about the number of people killed by their bathtubs was made up so everyone would buy one of those sticky mats, but now I'm not so sure. If all the ungrateful daughters of the world started littering their mother's tubs with loofahs, well you can see where that would lead. Oh, well, if it's not one thing it's another. If the cancer doesn't get you, bath products will.

I don't mean to go on like this, but let me ask you a question: who buys a loofah for an eighty year old woman? My skin is so thin that if I actually tried to exfoliate, I'd probably exfoliate myself right into the emergency room. At our age, just getting into the shower is enough to worry about. And remaining upright is a whole other thing. You know I have to keep my eyes open the entire time because if I close them I get the spins? Do you know what it's like not being able to close your eyes when the soap and shampoo start running?

So, anyway, Jenny says she feels bad, though I have my doubts. The perfect murder is one that looks like an accident, right? That's what Perry Mason used to say, so there you go.

At least I don't have to worry about them popping over to the house without calling first. One time her and her husband—Art, his name is—showed up while I was still sleeping, and they let themselves in and gobbled up all my frozen pizzas. He eats anything within his reach, which actually isn't that much because he's the size of a small sixth grader. I tower over him and I've been steadily shrinking for seven years. Is it wrong to hate your son in law? You know, when he calls me Mom, I spit up a little bit. Can you imagine that? Stuff starts actually rushing towards the surface like it does when I catch one of those programs on television where they're eating bugs.

Your only true friend,
B. A. Fisher

From the Archives
The Last Stop Bulletin

The Weather Front

Most of you were probably wakened by the tornado siren shrieking around five o'clock this morning. Of course, most of you who remember the last tornado that blew through here probably rolled over and went back to sleep. We are sorry to say that the 1991 "tornado" that twirled through here so benignly that the grandchildren made a game out of seeing who could get closest to it, bared little resemblance to the one that touched down this morning not ten miles from here, wiping out much of that new construction project over by the highway. Fortunately, the crews had yet to arrive, and nobody was hurt, but it did completely level the strip mall they were building. If you remember, that was the site of the old Grain Elevator that the historical society fought to save and lost. How's that for Karma?

Upcoming Events

He's done it. Against all odds, Nathan has done what no other man, woman or child has done before. Despite being verbally abused and physically assaulted with everything from measuring spoons to bags of flour, he has made it in Amato's kitchen for an entire week. He must feel a bit like Andy Bowen and Jack Burke after their 111 round boxing match. As the last seconds ticked away, Nathan smiled, ducked one last rolling pin, and made a hasty retreat to the time clock where family and friends were waiting with balloons and sponge cake. Even Amato was impressed. Mr. Cooper overheard him laughing softly and mumbling something about little bastards, which can only be positive. There will be a party tomorrow afternoon in the Activities Room to mark the occasion. Good for you, Nathan!

You Ought to Know

Let the game begin! Now that the weather has finally cooperated, the annual co-ed softball game between The Splinters and The Mighty Badgers will be played this afternoon. Harry is busy with the chalk lines, so please stay off the grass until game time. You know how he is about his chalk lines. Harry will also be replacing Ernie as Umpire. Ernie, we found out last year, calls every pitch a strike because he doesn't want to offend the pitcher, so the games is over in like three seconds. It turns out he can also be easily swayed by the female players and can be bribed with cigarettes. Harry isn't easily swayed by anything, even acts of God. And when Harry thinks about cigarettes, he thinks about the butts they turn into which are then littered all over our (which is to say his) precious grounds, so if you offer him one, you'll probably end up smoking it out of something other than your mouth. Incidentally, if there is anyone still puffing away, see Kelly. She has pictures of lungs and tongues that you might be interested in seeing.

The Hot Seat

As you know, Ernie HAD been taking his meals in the restaurant like the rest of us until SOMEONE commented on his using a spoon to eat his green beans and he hasn't been seen since. Marge spotted him eating a bag of Doritos by the vending machines this morning, so maybe he's turned the corner. As for the inconsiderate soul who forced his or her vast knowledge of proper eating techniques on unsuspecting Ernie, well, you know who you are.

THE SUGGESTION BOX

And speaking of Ernie, for the third time, it turns out (smile Ernie, you're a STAR!) Ernie (yes, Ernie) has spoken and we have listened. He has suggested that no one needs the healing effects of Holy Moses more than Mary Stuart and we agree, so Holy Moses will be unavailable evenings between seven and nine until Mary feels better. Mary loves each and every one of us, but her heart has always belonged to Moses. And now let's give Ernie a big round of applause. Good for you!

HOLY MOSES!

More ping pong balls are on order. Whoever introduced them to Holy should be ashamed of yourself. It wouldn't be so bad if he would return the balls to one of the players, but when he catches them he eats them and Harry is freaking out because he keeps finding plastic fragments in Holy's business. Besides, the way he tears after them puts everyone at risk. So, in the interest of safety and world peace, please make sure Holy has left the building before starting any matches. In the meantime, let's put our heads together and come up with a similar but suitable replacement toy. We have a feeling that he just wants to be involved, so the more interactive the better.

CASSANDRA

I usually don't come out here when it's this hot, but this new girl I'm training is driving me crazy. I just got promoted to Lead Nurse a few weeks ago, so I guess I need the practice, but she talks so much I can barely get a word in edgewise. I'm supposed to complete the tour in a little over an hour, and here it is quarter after ten, and we haven't even gone up to Special Care yet.

Oh, she's interested; she's just much more interested in other things. Everything I tell her reminds her of some cute anecdote about one of her previous jobs, or previous boyfriends, or previous lives, or her cat Sparkles who is mitten-toed and sleeps on her head and can't be trusted on cat nip.

When she does ask questions it's totally unrelated to her job. When I was showing her the medicine logs, she asked me how often Harry waters the grass. It's like she just says the first thing that pops into her head. Maybe it's because she's young. I'm young, too, but I can honestly say I've never wondered how often anybody waters their grass, and if I did, I certainly wouldn't wonder about it out loud.

If Missy, that's her name, had her way, she would line up everyone who ever lived so she could find out about everything that ever happened to anyone or anything in the whole history of the universe, but then she'd probably get distracted and ask a question only a beetle would have the answer to.

Anyway, she is very sweet, but I had to get away for a few minutes. I told her I was feeling nauseous and needed air, and she said she'd come out with me just in case I got sick so she could hold back my hair. You see? Sweet. I had to tell her to stay like seven times just like you would a new puppy. Luckily for me, she saw one of the painters and rushed to ask him what paint is made out of.

Her biggest problem is that she's single. I know this, because she told me two hundred different ways since she got here this morning. She broke up with Todd last night, and here it's been twelve hours and, oh my god, she's all alone, and always will be unless she acts fast. She spotted Nathan when he was punching in, so she's probably back there twirling her hair in his general direction. She's probably got the painters doing cartwheels. Set them up and knock them down.

Do I sound bitter? It's probably because I lived with HIM for so long. Prison is a good place for him. The only bad thing is that he's going to get out some day. He's not dangerous; he's an idiot. I should talk. I'm the one that stayed with him for so long. I was one of those silly girls, too. I thought having a complete jackass was better than having no jackass at all, but I'm through with all of that.

Oh, I forgot to tell you. Hold onto your seat. I'm going to teach myself the piano. I'm so excited. I'm going to run by Sears after my shift and buy a keyboard. No sense paying a fortune for an actual piano before I know if I have a knack for it. I'm so nervous. Can someone my age learn? You always hear about these people who are really good because they've been playing since they were four. My brother and I used to beat on cans with wooden spoons when we were kids, and I played the triangle in a fourth grade play, but I don't know if that counts—oh, Missy found me. Wish me luck.

ASTER

Does my breathing annoy you? I'm self conscience about it now, you see. That's what started the whole thing. You see that gentleman over there doing jumping jacks? I know you wouldn't think it to look at me, but me and that man came to blows once because of an argument I had with my wife concerning my breathing.

We were having our morning coffee like we've had every morning for four hundred years when she suddenly glared at me and said, "Do you have to breathe like that?"

"Yes dear," I said, "it's one of life's necessities, like food or water. You're a smart old gal, you should know that." I admit I said it a smidge sarcastically, but I think I hardly deserved her reply, which was, "You could stop breathing altogether." After forty years of marriage these kinds of things just roll off the tongue.

I should have stopped things there and went on with my crossword puzzle, but I was feeling feisty, and reveled in the thought of further provoking her.

"If you're suggesting that I breathe out my nose only," I told her. "I would be denying my abnormally large brain the oxygen it needs to function at full capacity. Besides, my nose whistles, you know that."

"The only thing abnormally large is your ears," she says.

We pride ourselves on our cruel wit, but it can still sting. We've done this sort of thing for years, taking little jabs at each other, but it's always been in fun, but that morning seemed different...meaner, maybe. I asked her, partly because it would annoy her, and partly because I was genuinely curious, "Why do you hate me all of a sudden?"

"If I hated you," she said calmly enough, "I would smother you in your sleep."

And that was that. She got up and walked—some might say stomped—into the kitchen, dumped her coffee into the sink, then, without another word, disappeared into the bedroom. Several minutes later, I watched her drag an overstuffed suitcase down the hallway to the front door, where she stopped and asked me if I could please get the door for her.

She has, I'll have you know, tried to smother me on at least three occasions. I mentioned that my nose whistles a moment ago, and so it does. I'm not ashamed of it. I read somewhere that there are African tribes that breed for it. At first, Ruby loved it. She called me her little whistler and we'd laugh, but as the years went on, I noticed that she was laughing less and less, and when I tried to whistle familiar melodies, which used to send her into hysterics, she looked at me as though she had suddenly smelled something foul. A decaying body, perhaps, or milk that's been left out in the sun.

I realize now that her hostility was because my nose was preventing her from sleeping at night. When I'm awake, you understand, I can generally control the volume and the tempo, but when I'm asleep, I have no control whatsoever. It got to be that she would leave the television on when we went to bed. One night I made the mistake of asking her if she could please turn it off because it was keeping me awake and she threw the alarm clock at me. If it hadn't been for the short cord, I might have ended up in the emergency room.

And one morning, a year or so later, I woke up on the floor with no recollection of how I had gotten there. I didn't concern myself with it too much. I just figured I had added sleepwalking to my repartee. I didn't put the pieces together until a few nights later when I was jarred awake by something hitting me in the face and neck and realized that my wife was battering me with, of all things, a lamp shade.

Later, after we both had sufficiently recovered to talk about what had happened, she said that she had been dreaming that she was surrounded by enormous, hairy, fanged spiders, and that I was their mother. Like in *Alien*, she said, only with spiders.

Ms. Fisher

Dearest Laverne:

Hold on to your mittens, I'm grouchy. Don't worry, the doctor, if you can really call him that, took the brunt of it. Doctor Kenneth Baker Jones, that's his name. His skin hasn't entirely cleared yet, and he wears these horn-rimmed glasses to try to hide the fact that he's an eight year old. I know its cliché, but he has a cowlick, Laverne. Do you see how annoying that is? If I ever have grandchildren, which I don't expect to—and considering the male half of that particular gene pool, I'm not really disappointed—I would push them into medicine. If they allow Doctor what's-his-ass to carry around a stethoscope and order people around twice his age, the profession must have lowered their standards considerably.

So he keeps telling me, "Don't worry, don't worry," over and over again like I'm a twelve year-old getting her tonsils out. And he keeps touching my arm and talking about the weather. You know how I am about strange people touching me. I finally took a swat at him, but I missed because he's young and quick. And later, when he interrupted my dinner and reached for my arm, I stabbed him with my fork. It didn't even break the skin. The fork was plastic, the big baby. I thought he was going to flop down on the floor and beat his little fists on the linoleum.

And speaking of tonsils, the girl on the other side of the curtain was recovering from that very thing. She wasn't doing any talking and I was bored so in an attempt to make conversation I told her that I had recently become frightened of infants. There is some truth to that, but I was mostly trying to get a laugh or something out of her. But since we're on the subject, I think what bothers me about babies is that they can't speak, so you never really know what they're thinking. Completely irrational, I know. I blame Stephen King. *Pet Semetery* scared me for life. The boy in the story wasn't an infant, mind you, but he never spoke once he came back from the dead, only growled, so you can see the connection. Give an infant a scalpel and you better be wearing high boots. Anyway, I told her all of this and she spilled it to Dr. Baby Cakes, so between that and stabbing him with the fork he's convinced that I have the beginning stages of dementia, if you can believe that.

After the fork thing, he started using one of his nurses as a go-between. I asked her why my roommate had suddenly disappeared, and she told me everything. She's one of these nurses you don't mess with, like Nurse Ratched in *One Flew Over the Cuckoo's Nest*, only she's really funny. We get along great. She doesn't like little Dr. Timmy Thumb Thumb anymore than I do, and she told me that if I was still there in the morning for breakfast, she'd make sure I got a real fork. We laughed and laughed.

Your only true friend,

B. A. Fisher

From the Archives
The Last Stop Bulletin

The Weather Front

Free at last! Free at last! Thank God Almighty, we are free at last! Looking out the window, it seems we've finally entered June. Mother Nature is off harassing the Midwest today, so unless we do something to tick her off, she'll be over there for the remainder of the week. She has a nasty habit of swinging back by just when we least expect it, though, so keep one eye on the sky. Eighty-eight will be the high today, with just enough of a breeze to keep things interesting.

You Ought to Know

Late in the ninth, the Splinters sent their best hitter and star left fielder Sue Gentry up to bat. The crowd hushed as she pointed to a clump of trees on the other side of the river and promptly hit a slow rolling grounder, which was easily scooped up by shortstop Henry who threw it to third base-woman Joan for a quick game of catch before lobbing it to Cicely at first base who was preoccupied filing her nails but still managed to catch the ball in time, sealing the victory for the Mighty Badgers. It wasn't, however, Sue's fault. Hank, pitcher and sometimes catcher, an odder combination you will not find, clearly threw the ball before Sue was ready, causing her to panic and hit the ball one-handed, ala tennis, which no doubt caused the scene just described, so we'll never know what the true outcome would have been. But when you're down eleven runs in the ninth, not even the Babe can save you.

More You Ought to Know

Pneumonia Spenonia. Chalk up another victory for Mary Stuart. It was a long fought battle, but late in the tenth, Mary turned it on strong, dusting off the old one-two and putting it to good use. The Battling P-monster came back with a flurry of desperate haymakers, but Mary ducked and bobbed and weaved until P-diddy dropped his guard and got caught with an uppercut that would have laid out Jack Dempsey! The ferocious P-ickle's legs wobbled and the eyes lulled. The mighty P-pod knew it had been licked and sunk quietly to the mat for a slow ten count. Come back some other day, silent P weirdo, and try again if you dare, but she is back and stronger than ever. We're not sure what the P thing is all about. It's been a weird morning.

The Hot Seat

We would like to take this opportunity to publically humiliate those of you who fell asleep during yesterday's game. You can talk all day about how draining the heat is, but you'll get nowhere with us. So, here they are, in no particular order: Ray Vector, Cynthia Paterson, Clive Henderson, Papa Diego, Jimmy Caster, and Sally Jensen. We don't mean to harp on you Ray, but some of us were offended when you exclaimed early in the second inning, "For god's sake, throw the ball, Robert! Some of us will be dead soon." For some, god's sake should be reserved for more pressing matters than softball, and despite the statistics, none of us will be dead soon, if ever. The remark, we're sure you remember, flustered Robert to such a degree that the ball went straight up and then straight back down onto the crown of his head, earning him seven stitches. After a heated debate, we have decided that you should be present for their removal.

The Suggestion Box

You have spoken and we have listened. We agree that it is not fair that Amato hog one of the computers all evening, and we have spoken, raised our voices, and yelled at him to give others a chance, but he threatened us with a dutch oven and reminded us that it isn't wise to anger the one preparing your food, so we aren't inclined to push it much farther. We have, however, posted a particularly angry-looking sign that reads "One Hour Limit!"

On a similar note, Mr. Jenkins is offering a beginner computer course next week. He will be bringing a projector this time, so you won't have to try and decipher his drawings.

As for Amato, don't confront him. He has a bad case of misdirected aggression, usually found in hyenas and house cats, and we don't want to give Nathan any more trouble. He's hanging on by his teeth.

HOLY MOSES!

It was bound to happen sooner or later. Holy finally figured out that it's easier to belly up to the buffet and take what he wants then it is to make rounds looking for handouts. So, alas, Holy-the-incredible-Moses will no longer be allowed to dine with us. Before anyone starts screaming and throwing little angry notes at Reception, we have thought about raising the buffet tables but this is unfair to our height challenged residents. If anyone has any suggestions, we're all ears. We all love him, even when he drools, but we have a budget to consider, not to mention the integrity of our food.

CASSANDRA

How are they making out? Holy appears to be winning. He always does and they never learn. Baths get him worked up. When they try to rinse him, he'll start knocking them down like bowling pins. I think he has a fear of drowning from when he was a puppy. That's why they want a couple of us out here. We're the first responders if something goes wrong. The funny thing is that as soon as they're done, Holy will take off and throw himself into the nearest dirt pile just to see the look on their faces.

So, they prepare for bath day by playing out different disaster scenarios with a stuffed lion. One of these days they're going to realize that making a circle around a stuffed lion and making a circle around Holy Moses are two very different things, and that waving towels only annoys him. They underestimate Holy's ability to find the weakest link. My money is on Ernie, the one on the end there. He's already jumpy and they have barely started. Want to put a wager on it? My prediction is that Ernie goes down within the next three minutes.

So I got my keyboard…It's got a built in program that teaches you songs. The keys light up as it plays so you can follow along. It also came with a bunch of stickers so you can label all the keys with the proper notes. The first song is *Twinkle Twinkle Little Star*. Did you catch the excitement in my voice? Twinkle is not Mozart and I can't play it to save my life. I had this crazy idea that I might be a natural. I figured I would sit down, play a few notes to familiarize myself with where they are, and then just play. I tried that…the sound that came out would stand your hair on end. I tried running up the keyboard like you see them doing and I actually jammed the middle finger on my left hand.

So now that I know I'm not a natural, I have to actually learn and I can already tell it's going to be crazy hard. Chords, pedal tones, octaves… there's even proper hand positioning, which makes me play even worse, which I didn't think was possible.

And then to top it off, I had a dream that I was doing a recital right here in the theater and the whole audience was clapping and weeping and throwing flower petals, and suddenly they were gone and Mozart was sitting in the front row and you know what he said to me? "Wood." Just that one word and I woke up screaming.

I'm not giving up, though. Tonight I'll have another go at *Songs for Preschoolers*. It's so humiliating. I don't know why I'm bothering with it, but there must be some reason they want you to learn it or they wouldn't have included it, right?

And Ernie's down! I told you, as soon as they got the hose near his face. "Stay down, Ernie!" I better go check on him; it looked like he landed weird.

ASTER

And there it is! Bravo! I knew it was only a matter of time before Byron realized he had an audience. That man is simply incapable of keeping his shirt on when there are spectators. One Christmas Eve, he stripped his shirt off right in the middle of the choir's rendition of *Oh Child of Bethlehem*. Coincidentally, the next song was *Come Let Us Adore Him* and the imbecile actually launched into some interpretive dance.

There are a few things you need to know about our friend Byron. He is known to drop down and do pushups unexpectedly, so it is wise to give him plenty of room if you find yourself walking behind him. Also, if you wander down to the picnic area, watch where you're walking. Byron makes a habit of sunbathing nude directly on the path, giving you no choice but to step over him or brave the sticker bushes. Other times, you will find the path unobstructed and will continue on with a spring in your step only to round the final corner and find him perched on top of one of the picnic tables like a human pelican.

All of this is harmless, but if he perceives a threat to his manhood, he becomes enraged, and his behavior becomes unpredictable. By way of example, the other day, an agreeable fellow named Lawrence was on one of the stationary bikes in the Fitness Center, really pushing himself, and Byron, who happened to walk in and notice this gross display of manliness, immediately hopped on one of the other bikes and took off at such a clip that his feet and knees were but blurs. And to complete the performance, he somehow managed to remove his shirt while waving one hand high above his head, lest there be any doubt about who had won the race. Lawrence, having learned from similar experiences in the Activities Room, smartly exited stage left, leaving Byron to bask in the glow of his own idiocy.

Now that we've spoken about the physical Byron, let's turn our attention to the intellectual Byron. It's hard to tell from here, but if you look closely you will notice that his brain is roughly the size and shape of a sunflower seed. If you ask him about books, he will try to distract you by flexing his calve muscle. If that doesn't work, he'll begin flipping his hair around and picking at it with the thick black comb he keeps tucked in his waistband. And if you still try to engage him in some form of intelligent conversation, he'll get you in a full nelson and drive you face first into the ground.

But enough about Byron! You're probably wondering what happened with Ruby, the first and better half of the unfolding drama. At last we left her she was dragging a suitcase off into the distance. She had threatened this very thing a few times over the course of our marriage, but to actually see it played out, left me speechless and unable to move.

The stories you tell yourself in times of stress range from the amusing to the grotesque. I spent the next several hours telling myself that it was all an elaborate hoax, and I laughed out loud. Any minute she will come back and we will have great big laugh. Ha, ha, ha. When the evening news came on and she still wasn't home, I told myself that she must have had a trip planned. Perhaps she had forgotten to tell me about it, or perhaps she had told me and I had forgotten. You see how ridiculous this gets? But when the truth is painful it is elusive. I believed all of this nonsense in one version or another all the way up until late the following afternoon when three reliable sources told me that they had spotted Ruby and our friend over there towel drying each other after spending the morning swimming together.

MS. FISHER

Dearest Laverne:

Hurray! I've been sprung. They tried their best to hold me, but my tests thus far have showed nothing to be alarmed about, so, for the time being, I'm free from the clutches of that little mouse of a doctor. You know, I flipped him the bird on the way out? That'll teach him to touch people that don't want to be touched.

When I got in this morning, there was a plate of cookies waiting for me at Reception. Beverly said that someone left them on her desk with a little note saying to make sure I got them. I am not without enemies, so I checked them for fuses and had Harry go over them with his metal detector. Just to be safe, I took them to our chef, Amato, to see if everything looked and smelled all right. His eyes lit up when I said they might be poisoned, but he said they appeared to be cookies wrapped in cellophane. I tried to get him to taste one, but he laughed and waggled his finger at me.

I should assume that they're from Jen. But here's the problem: these cookies appear to be delicious, and Jen doesn't bake. She doesn't cook, clean, do laundry or have manners, either, since we're on the subject. If they looked and smelled like burnt toaster strudel, then there would be no mystery. The other thing bothering me is that if she did bake them herself, she might end up killing me unintentionally. How's that for a Greek Tragedy? I don't know. You can't be too careful when your daughter is married to someone named Art. If your last name isn't Garfunkel, I don't want to hear about it.

Perhaps I'm still bitter. Did I ever tell you about Oprah? If I did, you're just going to have to grin and get through it. I'll know if you skip ahead. A couple of years ago, I had to go out of town for the weekend so I had Jenny stay at the house. Earlier that week I had caught one of my drug addict neighbors eyeballing my pelicans, and you can never be too careful. Anyway, Jenny saw a show Oprah did about simplifying your life by removing all the unnecessary clutter. So, instead of removing the clutter from her own life, starting with her husband, she decided to practice by removing the clutter from my life. When I got back, almost everything was gone. Laverne, she sold everything but the furniture: dishes, my beloved books, knickknacks, my clothes…You know me, I'm not usually short on words, but all I could say was, "What have you done?"

"You didn't want any of those old things, mother," she says. "I've never seen you wear any of those things."

"You're never around to see me wear any of those things!" It was terrible, the whole thing. And you want to know the kicker? Somebody made off with my damn pelicans.

Your only true friend,

B. A. Fisher

FROM THE ARCHIVES
THE LAST STOP BULLETIN

THE WEATHER FRONT

E.B. White once said that weather is a great bluffer, and we couldn't agree more. We would add that Ma Nature is moody and not above breaking out the wooden spoon. But we are happy to report that her and her spoon are headed north towards the Great Lakes. She won't be back by to check on us until late tomorrow afternoon, so go crazy. It's going to be hot, though, so if you're going to go outdoors, stop by Reception and grab some sun block. Beverly collects the free samples that come in the mail. She collects other things, too, but in the name of decency, we will refrain.

UPCOMING EVENTS

We will be having a guest speaker Thursday evening. His name is Geoffrey Bloomer (we're not kidding) and he will be giving his lecture, "Balance, What is it Good for?" We aren't sure what it's about, but we've heard it's riveting…

We have sent an apology to Mr. Hayman, last month's speaker, whom you pelted with raisins until he turned red-faced and stormed out. Okay, okay, his talk "Stem-cells in the Duck, How are they Different?" was a bit dry, but throwing food? We promised the Board we'd bring the hammer down so here goes: You should be ashamed of yourselves! The Board would also like to remind you that if raisins are thrown with enough force and at the right angle, they can take out someone's eye.

The Board, however, is not who you should be frightened of; it's Harry who has to pick them up one at a time because "The damn things can't be swept!" The weird weather has really gotten to him this summer so please, if you must throw something, make sure you find it and dispose of it after the speech is over. We have high hopes for Mr. Bloomer, but the more we think about it, the title isn't very promising. We are still trying to get Stephen King in for a signing, but no official word yet. We'll keep you posted.

You Ought to Know

Head Health Care Nurse, Barb Watson, thinks she is going to leave us for a better paying, less stressful job at the Federal Center. We think not. She is, as you know, much too good to let go of that easily. So we want all of you to go out of your way to shower her with hugs and good cheer. We have a backup plan that involves chains and duct tape, but we hope it doesn't come to that.

The Hot Seat

If you have young children nearby, you might want to send them to the store for ice…After much discussion we have come to the conclusion that after a woman reaches a certain age—eighty -one last May, for example—she should keep her breasts to herself. And if she insists on wearing those low cut, semi see-through blouses with the red polka dots placed oh so carefully…oh, all right, we'll just say it: Ms. Theron, while we are all secretly in ah of your figure this late in life, we must insist that you cover up the girls when you're outside your room. Honestly, how you have denied gravity and all of nature to get them to stand up like that without some kind of pulley system is beyond all comprehension. There was a pile up of old men yesterday trying to get a look at you in the new Yoga class, and they almost started rioting. Order must be restored.

And since we're on the topic and seem to be on a roll: We all know about the time you spent in the presidential suite at the Brown Palace with Mr. Roosevelt talking (ha, ha) politics, so there is no need to repeat it at every sit-down. We are envious, take our word for it.

THE SUGGESTION BOX

You have spoken and we have listened. Some of you have expressed concern that the sneeze guards in the restaurant aren't adequate because some of our shorter residents can duck under them. Well, we're sorry, but the current sneeze guards are here to stay. They have been up for twenty-five years and no one has died yet. And yes, we know all about flu season, so if you feel a sneeze is unavoidable, turn and stifle it in the crook of your arm. We're all adults here.

HOLY MOSES!

It has been brought to our attention that a three year old Alaskan Malamute named Ricky living in Boise has the largest documented vocabulary of any living canine. He reportedly recognizes and understands one hundred and eighty-seven words. Considering that there are 670 different types of cheeses, we are confident that our boy can shatter the record and send Ricky back to pulling sleds.

The record must be set straight. Holy Moses is the most extraordinary canine to ever live, and it's about time the world knows it. So, the first step is to find out what Holy's current vocabulary is, and then expand on it with the use of synonyms. Beverly will post a running list on the Community Board, so check it often and make sure you're reinforcing the new words. You can try teaching him tricks to go along with the new words, but remember that Holy only does what Holy feels like doing so proceed at your own peril.

CASSANDRA

Screw *Itsy Bitsy Spider*, that's all I'm saying. I actually started having flashbacks from kindergarten when Lucinda Spinney pushed me down in the sand and shoved paste up my nose. Do you know what it's like reliving that over and over again? Who wants to hear that song, anyway? And *Pop goes the Weasel*? I don't even know what that means. Did someone put him in the microwave?

Anyway, it doesn't matter. I heard this song called *Moonlight Sonata* on the classical station and I looked it up online and I can actually play the first fifteen seconds of it. It's so beautiful. I almost cried when I heard it and I don't even know why.

Believe it or not, I had heard of Beethoven, but I wasn't sure if he was a composer or a writer. Now I know. He's no Mozart, but I want to hug him for writing a song that I can at least partially play. It might be hard, though, because I looked him up, too, and he's been dead a really long time.

Look at my fingers. I was up until three in the morning playing it. They're better now, but when I got up this morning, they were locked in a claw. It took ten minutes of straightening them to get them to where they wouldn't spring back when I let go. Can you imagine if they stayed that way? I'd be like Max Schreck in Nosferatu.

So I've got the first fifteen seconds down and it sounds amazing. And if that's all I'm ever able to play, then fine, at least I can say, "Yes, I play a little Beethoven," and be telling the truth. Now if I could just play a little Mozart. The scary thing is that there's going to come a time when someone's going to want me to play something for them. My palms get all sweaty just thinking about, so don't even think about spreading this around. I know where you live.

I'd play it for you sometime, but my luck you would turn out to be some retired virtuoso and when I got done you'd say, "That's great, but I can play it with my feet."

ASTER

I realize now that I panicked. After hearing the news of Ruby and Byron's pool adventures, I spent all of the next morning lurking in the Fitness Center, trying to catch them in the throngs of some passionate embrace among the dumbbells. To stay partially hidden, I entangled myself in the various exercise machines, which, I thought at the time, must be torture devices inspired by Caligula. At one point, one of the cables had so completely ensnared my collar that I was unable to free myself without first taking my shirt off. I then spent the next several minutes tugging on it while a crowd of onlookers gathered to snicker and make wisecracks.

I'm afraid the humiliation didn't end there. Since I was already half nude, I borrowed Ernie's snorkel and spent the next three hours partially submerged like a nuclear submarine patrolling enemy waters. Three hours is an awfully long time to soak, and when I got out, a different crowd began cracking off about flounders and ironing boards. In their defense, I don't think they were aware of the facts surrounding my actions. Had they known the details, I'm sure they would have refrained from harassing me. They may have even offered me a towel, which, in my agitated state, I had forgotten.

I don't know how quickly word spread about Byron and Ruby, but on the way back to my room several people greeted me with a barely perceptible shake of the head and a sympathetic smile. Of course, this may have been a reaction to the way my clothes were adhered to my body at weird angles or how my hair clumped and jutted out to one side.

Once back in my room, I spent the greater part of an hour peeling off my wet clothes and drying myself. It was during this time that I realized that the green blouse that had been hanging on the bathroom door that morning was gone, as were the silver hoop earrings that had been lying on the dresser. Obviously, while I was busy snorkeling in a lifeless body of water, Ruby had returned to the room to gather up more of her things. Now, this may not seem like such a big deal, but how will you react when I tell you that Ruby only wore that blouse and those earrings when we were out on romantic occasions?

There it is! That's the reaction I was looking for. It took you a minute, but if you would have added the sudden urge to vomit to you performance, you would have mirrored my reaction exactly.

So, I did what anyone would have done in my shoes. I removed the seven or eight bottles of liquor we kept in a cabinet above the sink and set about deciding which bottle I would drink first. Now, my intention was to drink just enough to dull the senses, but intentions should never be mixed with alcohol. By the end of the first hour, I was making up folk songs with Ruby as the main theme. By hour two, I had lost the ability to think rationally and could no longer come up with lyrics that resembled English, so I set about dancing to the music in my head. By the time the sun went down, I had lost the motor skills necessary for walking or even standing. At some point during all of this, I wrote down a plan of action. I keep this with me as a reminder of how quickly you can go from a decent, rational, intelligent human being, to a raving lunatic if the right set of circumstances show up. So here it is. I have left it completely unabridged and unedited…

Ms. Fisher

Dearest Laverne:

I threw the cookies out just to be on the safe side. My stomach has been bothering me a bit lately, and one of Jen's cookies, even if they aren't poisoned, might be enough to put me right back in the hospital. I'm not safe, though. I caught a glimpse of Art, my daughter's dumb husband, prowling around the parking lot. I'm sure it was him. Once you've seen him, the image stays with you like a picture of a two-headed cow. He's always popping up when you least expect it, the sneaky SOB. At the end of the world, all there will be is cockroaches and Art. And when he's not eating them, he'll probably be mating with them, fathering some super-species that will dominate the earth until the next asteroid hits.

I couldn't tell where he went. I lost him between two parked cars. The last I saw was the top of his bald, scaly head bobbing as he walked and then he was gone. He probably dropped down on all fours to try and peek up women's dresses. Either that or he attached himself to the undercarriage of the transport van like that loony in *Cape Fear*. You remember that? What an awful movie. The first one was bad enough, but I've never been able to look at Robert De Niro the same after seeing him in the second one. Even in *Meet the Parents*, all I saw was Max Cady with his fingers in that poor girl's mouth. Oh, it gives me the heebie-jeebies just thinking about it. He did die in the end, though, so that makes me happy.

Strange that Art was out during the day, though. I didn't think bloodsuckers could be exposed to sunlight. You may laugh, but the jury is still out on that one. I have a photo—I'll send it to you because I know you won't believe me—of Jen and Art sitting by the fireplace on Christmas Eve, and Art's staring at the fire with this deranged look on his face. Who gets that worked up about fire? Explain that, if you don't mind. I bet pyromaniacs don't even look like that. And that's not the worst of it. His eyes are red and he's got one hand behind his back like he's hiding a meat cleaver or something, and everything below his waist is foggy. And don't talk to me about double exposures or any other such nonsense, because everything else in the picture is crystal clear, and besides I'm no stranger to picture-taking. I took a class on it in the late seventies, so your baseless explanations will get nowhere with me. I've got a bucket full of holy water I've been saving for just such an occasion, so if he makes a move, I'll douse him with it and listen to him crackle and pop.

Your only true friend,
B. A. Fisher

From the Archives
The Last Stop Bulletin

The Weather Front

We have officially set a record! We only wish it was a good record. As it stands, yesterday we beat the heat record for the year 1907 of ninety-three by almost six degrees, and we don't need Ms. Farley on the nine o'clock news to tell us it is going to be hot again today. Ladies and Gentlemen, say hello to the dog days of August, they've arrived early, and they didn't even bring cheese cake.

Upcoming Events

Cover your ears. The Stamina Stairs are officially closed, per Mary Stuart, effective immediately. For the three of you who don't know the stairs of which we speak, it is the set that climbs steeply from the garden to the second floor bedroom of the original house.

Everyone agrees that climbing stairs is a good cardiovascular exercise and a great way to test your overall conditioning, but the fact is those stairs are too steep, too narrow, and too old to be used as an Olympic apparatus. If you don't believe us, get with Ed and he can tell you all about how the railing gave way three steps from the top, leaving him dangling 20 feet above the geraniums. If you need more of a visual, think of Harold Lloyd in *Safety Last*.

Thankfully, Harry can now add Mountain Rescue to his resume

without fudging too much. Some may question his use of a steel garden rake as a means of hooking Ed's shirt collar and hauling him in, but we applaud Harry for being resourceful. Ed did sustain some blunt force trauma to the head and collarbone, but those wounds will heal. Oh, and yes, we know this doesn't really qualify as an event, but it had to go somewhere so leave us alone.

YOU OUGHT TO KNOW

Keeping with the dismal tone of today's Bulletin, we have more bad news. Despite Holy's attempts at healing Mary Stuart, she has taken a bad turn and is spending some time with the good people at Swedish Medical Center. She reported having trouble breathing during the night, and this morning her blood pressure was dangerously low. We don't have visitor information yet, but we will by tomorrow. We might shuttle groups down to see her, though this may prove to be too stressful for her. We'll keep you posted. In the meantime, there is a card in Reception. Holy has taken this personally, so shower him with hugs when you see him.

THE HOT SEAT

Please, please, please Ms. Crocker. We know you read this. It is not acceptable to leave a trail of nuts and berries to your bedroom windowsill. You are attracting all sorts of "little" critters that aren't so little. Need we remind you that there are bears in the area, not to mention coyotes and angry raccoons? Furthermore, Ms. Crocker, we like Elk, everybody does; we just aren't fond of herds, so please, we must insist that you stop this at once. We are not running a zoo, no matter what people think.

THE SUGGESTION BOX

You have spoken and we have listened. It has been brought to our attention that while everyone loves Holy Moses there are some of you who grew up with cats and miss the aloofness and general disdain. We also know that there are some who have such a deep-rooted fear of cats, that just the sight of them has you jumping out windows. Those of you here long enough will remember that most of us had the same reaction to Holy Moses when he came bounding down the hallway, and now he's a celebrity, so it's not unreasonable to think that there might be some equally extraordinary cat sitting in one of the humane societies that would fill the role nicely. Ultimately, of course, it will be up to Holy Moses, because, after all, he was here first.

Holy Moses!

Alert! Alert! Bath team! Code Red! Holy Moses spent the morning rolling in some unknown substance down by the river and now he's busy stinking up every corner of the building. The good news is that with the crazy heat lately, Holy has been spending more and more time parked over one of the sprinkler heads, so your work is half done. Have your buckets and shampoo ready, and make sure you're rested. For those of you new to the bath team, we must warn you that water does funny things to him, so he might suddenly take flight or playfully (though painfully) mouth your arm. While he's still wet, be cautious when opening any of the exterior doors. He's big, but somehow he's sneaky. Also, there is a good possibility that he will make a break for the unknown substance once he's clean just out of spite, so you'll need to form some kind of human wall.

CASSANDRA

I don't have long because I have to get up and see Mr. Robertson. He's gone on strike. He says he won't eat or drink unless I bath him. I'm serious. He was just moved up to Special Care a couple of months ago because Harry found him wading in the river and he couldn't remember how he had gotten there. He just turned ninety-three last week, and since Franklin died, he's been acting out. Franklin was his best friend. They used to play chess every evening at nine o'clock. They played every night for fifteen years, and then Franklin got sick and it turned out to be stomach cancer, and…Mr. Robertson hasn't been the same since. The first week he played chess by himself but talked to Franklin like he was there.

Anyway, he threw his water on Shelby, one of the new nurses, and last week he started singing *Moon River* at the top of his lungs all day and night until he lost his voice. Now he's refusing to eat or drink, and coming up with all sorts of demands, one of which is me bathing him. He doesn't really expect me to, he just wants me up there. I'm one of his favorites. He calls me Apples because he says Peaches is cliché.

So, you'll never guess what I got in the mail. Do you remember a while back when I was telling you about my convict boyfriend and how he was going to get out one day? Well, surprise, it's going to be sooner than I thought. I got a letter from him this morning, talking about how he's changed and how I'm the only one he's ever loved, blah, blah, blah. I don't even think he wrote it because the handwriting was legible and he didn't use the word baby once. Oh, and at the end, you know what he tells me? That he quit smoking cigarettes. He was drunk before breakfast, cheated on me at least three times that I know of, got busted for selling hash to an undercover, and punched one of the arresting officers who just happened to be a woman. Yes, jackass, the smoking is what concerns me.

He didn't say when he's getting out, but he's counting the seconds—probably on his toes—and he can't stop thinking about me. "My heart aches for you, baby." He didn't say that, but it's exactly like something he would say. It's all lies, anyway. He knows I'm the only one who can help him. If he shows up at my door I don't know what I'm going to do, but I promise you it'll be something very unlike me.

Thanks for not laughing at me the other night. I played even worse than I thought I would, which is encouraging. It *was Moonlight Sonata*, I swear. I can't believe how nervous I was. How do you get stage freight playing in front of one person?

Anyway, Vernon—that's his name: Vernon with a V he tells people—has inspired me to learn the *Halloween* theme song. Isn't that twisted? It's not like I light candles and sharpen knives or anything, but it gives me a weird sort of pleasure when I think about him while I'm playing it…I'm not sure that's healthy.

ASTER

1. *Gather intelligence. Like in any war, you need to know what you're up against. How deep is she in? Is she just trying to make me jealous, or is it something more? Is it possible that she actually sees something in Byron? Is it possible that Byron is able to provide her with something that I cannot? What does the missing green blouse and earrings signify? Is it serious or just a one-night stand—*

2. *Stakeout Byron's room in hopes of catching them coming or going. Check the door. If open and all seems quiet, do not hesitate to snoop. Check the bathroom and bedroom for signs of extended stay. Check the cupboards for overstocked food, and the refrigerator for cheap wine. If caught, do not confront them, I repeat, do not confront them. If surprised, trip him and run away. If met with open arms, stay for tea and jam toast.*

3. *Recruit spies. This will be tricky. No way of knowing if she's gotten to them first. Ask around. Someone somewhere knows something about sometime... This is a great big country with lots of foreigners to pick from. Check government website for CIA strategies and techniques. Check library for the movie The Saint with Val Kilmer in case disguises are needed. If possible, find out who did Val's makeup. If all fails, reach out to Val himself. He seems like a good guy.*

4. *If there is a way to…yes, do that. Don't go back, though! Too dangerous. If there are spiders, recruit them, too, and wasps…Monopoly might solve the whole thing. Take all their houses and leave them desti-tute and alone with not even a kitten to play with.*

I won't comment. I should note that I vomited at the conclusion of the first item. That's the one thing that stands out with any clarity. It's amazing how certain word combinations used in the right context can evoke a physical response. The rest is so appalling that it speaks for itself. It's a good reminder, though. We all need reminders: little things that help us from going off the deep end in the future. Mark Twain once said, "A man that carries a cat by its tail learns something he can learn in no other way." This is my cat.

The next morning is one I won't soon forget: full of dry heaving and purple spots and an insane chirping that I thought was in my head but turned out to be a nest of robins outside my window. Edgar Allen Poe spoke of the senses becoming acute during times of stress, but for me they are at their most sensitive while in the throngs of a hangover. I heard everything: the faucet dripping, the aforementioned screaming birds, the refrigerator clicking, Holy Moses bathing himself four doors down, everything in blaring stereo. I was such a ghastly shade of white that I had to shield my eyes from my reflection. And I could actually feel my hair, which is kind of like seeing air.

But wounded most deeply was my ego. Educated men don't make a habit out of blurring fantasy and reality. They don't wake up at the kitchen table with their shirt off and their shoes on. And they certainly don't ring up Val Kilmer at three o'clock in the morning. Against all odds, there was someone named Val Kilmeir in the phone book with whom I apparently had a long conversation about stamp collecting.

Ms. Fisher

Dearest Laverne:

Is it hot where you are? It's miserable here. This weather makes me crazy. I know we're supposed to have the greatest weather on the planet, something like 300 days of sunshine, but they don't mention that with the sunshine comes heat that is unbearable unless you're parked right next to an air conditioner, which I refuse to do because it dries out my nose.

I prefer to be outside, but when it's 90 degrees at ten o'clock in the morning, I just can't bring myself to do it, so I usually deal myself a few hands of solitaire or play cards with Ms. Hathaway from down the hall. She's a cheater, though. She knows it and I know it. There is absolutely no way any one person can be that lucky. The game doesn't matter. I challenged her to War one time just to throw her off, but she still handed me my backside inside of ten minutes. I did beat her once at Hearts, though, after she was dealt the worst hand in the history of the game, but even then if I wouldn't have held tight to the queen of spades, she would have shot the moon. Both of us were so stunned by the outcome that neither one of us said a word. If I could have that moment back, I would do a little dance and yell obscenities, but I was too dumfounded at the time. Since then, she spends most of her time scribbling in the little notebook she carries around. I know she's perfecting her Hearts strategy, because I catch her consulting her notebook while she plays on the computer. We haven't played since, and I don't plan on it, either. I have beaten the hustler Hathaway at her favorite game. Now I can die with a smile on my face.

Rumor has it that she and her husband, now deceased, used to play nine-ball at the local pool halls. Hathaway would wheel up to one of the tables, playing every bit the frail old lady, while her husband tried to find someone who would play her for fifty bucks. When the game started, of course, she would miraculously spring from her wheelchair, spin her cue like a Japanese war staff, and clear the table. They were even on ESPN one time demonstrating trick shots.

She still plays the frail old lady here. I know she doesn't need the chair, but I'm not mean enough to dump her out of it just to prove it. I bet at night she ditches it and does one-armed pushups while watching Jeopardy. Good for her, though, that's what I say. She's just trying to stay sharp. Everyone needs something to work on. Hers just happens to be making us look silly at the card table. At our age, you need projects. Things that keep you up at night, and make you want to wake up in the morning. If you don't, you'll start really getting old, and before you know it, you'll be up on the third floor. My goal is to never end up in Special Care. I'd much prefer gorking over while having a swim or eating my tomato poppers with ranch. Wouldn't that be something? I can just see Kelly, our fitness instructor, standing over my lifeless body shaking her head, saying, "I told you to stay away from the ranch dressing."

The Specials make me so sad. Not many start out in Assisted and then end up in Special Care. Most of them were brought here because they became too much to handle. Their children have their own lives. I understand that. What an awful feeling, though, that you are somehow hurting your children by continuing to live...If Jennifer doesn't shape up, I'm going to live forever.

Your only true friend,

B. A. Fisher

From the Archives
The Last Stop Bulletin

The Weather Front

Who needs weather people when the parking lot pavement is melting and the lawn is crispy and painful to walk on, even despite Harry's End Days Watering Schedule. It's hot and will remain so until it's not any more. So there. These weather reports are becoming tiresome lately. If you happen to see a cloud, blink three times really fast, and if it's still there, hurry to Reception so Beverly can snap a picture of it.

Upcoming Events

Starting today at noon and continuing until six, Randy will be shuttling groups of ten to visit Mary Stuart at Swedish Medical Center. She is not doing well, and is heavily sedated, but she is conscious and we know she would love to see all of you. Due to our remarkable math skills, we have deduced that because of the small group size, not everyone will be able to make it today, so we have canceled tomorrow's trip to the mall to give everyone a chance to see her.

You Ought to Know

The air conditioning is back on! Thanks to our fearless Man of all Trades, who worked through the night to restore forced air, we can all put away those ridiculous hats with the little fans attached to them. Thank You Harry! And thank YOU for leaving Harry to his work. There were no out of the ordinary injuries reported, so you must have learned from experience.

THE HOT SEAT

Well, Ms. Crocker, you've done it. Three different people have now spotted what can only be a black bear hanging out just beyond our property line down by the river. It should only be a matter of days before he starts plucking us from our beds. We hope you're happy!

THE SUGGESTION BOX

You have spoken and we have listened. Whoever suggested that Amato is spending so much time on the computer because he's looking at French porn should be ashamed of herself (the writing was distinctly female.) Amato is a happily married man, god help her. He has some nasty habits, but pornography is definitely not one of them. Recipes are what he's after. He may have come upon something by accident, but we're sure it was completely unintentional. Besides, he's getting better about sharing. It only took three of us to drag him away yesterday. He was once again yelling about the "Stinking Leper Stew" but he calmed down once he was back in his kitchen.

HOLY MOSES!

Holy's nails are officially out of control. You can hear his nails clicking on the floor from outer space. So, nail team, we know you've been putting it off, but you're on deck. Keep in mind that Holy knows what the nail trimmers look like, where they are kept, and the facial expression of someone trying to hide them from him, so you'll need to plan ahead. Once he realizes what is happening, you will want to wrap him in a sturdy blanket, feed him Doritos, and sing to him until the job is done. If you hit the quick, however, no one, not even God, can help you.

One other thing: Holy Moses shares Harry's dislike for ladders, especially when there are strange people crawling around on them, so let's all work together in keeping him away from the painters.

CASSANDRA

Do you believe in ghosts? I just thought I'd ask since I saw one a few minutes ago. Sorry, I shouldn't have sprung that on you. Let me back up. Three years ago, my grandmother got sick and I went to visit her in the hospital. On my way up to her room, I saw this little girl in a cute yellow dress getting off the elevator as I was getting on. No big deal, right? But when I got off the elevator on the eleventh floor, I saw her again up on her tippy toes trying to drink out of the water fountain. Freaky, I know. But it gets worse. I realized that I was on the wrong floor, so I got back on the elevator and when the doors opened on the tenth floor, the same little girl was sitting on the couch twirling her hair.

When I told this to my mom, she explained that the little girl must have taken the stairs up to the eleventh floor and then stopped for a drink of water because she was thirsty from having just run up eleven flights of stairs before turning around and riding the handrail back down to the tenth floor where she threw herself on the couch, obviously exhausted. And besides, she said, she couldn't have been a ghost because she looked normal and she wasn't sticking her tongue out or holding a hatchet. I then turned to my grandmother, who, even in her weakened state, had a much more reasonable explanation. She said that they were obviously twin girls who were dressed the same and that I just happened to run into both of them.

I believed that. But here's the problem. I just saw that same little girl sitting out on the lawn. She was wearing the same yellow dress and she was mocking me by singing *Twinkle Twinkle Little Star*. Seriously, I would have screamed, but I like to think I'm a grown woman. Besides, she's gone now. I can't wait to see where she pops up next. At least now I can scratch "see a ghost or demon" off my bucket list.

So for more good news, somehow Vernon with a V has found out where I work. Beverly says he's been calling twice a day. I told her not to accept any calls. If someone really needs to get a hold of me, they can call my cell phone, and if she gives him that number they'll have to troll for her body in the river. But the good news is that he's been calling at ten and at four every day, which tells me they haven't let him out yet. Beverly thinks I should talk to him. She says he doesn't sound like a criminal at all. I love Beverly, truly I do, but she thought the fish were plastic—I shouldn't say that. She's great and Vernon with a V can actually be really charming and funny when he's not being a total idiot. Whatever. I don't know what's worse: being stalked by a dead girl or an ex boyfriend who calls himself Vernon with a V.

The *Halloween* theme song was coming along but it's officially on hold until SHE goes away. No sense encouraging her. She looks sweet enough but that music does funny things to people. I was trying to learn it by ear because sheet music makes me physically ill when I look at it. I gave up trying to learn the rest of *Moonlight Sonata* for exactly that reason. The beginning is the only part that matters anyway.

I'm thinking about getting an actual piano. I know I stink, but I think I would stink less if I was playing something nice. At least then, all the wrong notes would have a nice ring to them. They're really expensive, though. I figure if I start saving now I'll have one by the summer of 2027. Maybe I can find a used one somewhere. Know anyone with a piano for sale for about fifty bucks? I know, I'll tell Vernon about it and he'll steal one for me, then I could stash the piano and turn him in. It's perfect. I'd have my piano, and Vernon would be back to taking showers with his back against the wall...sorry, that was inappropriate—oh, what do you care? You think I'm a nut anyway.

ASTER

Afraid I'm under the weather today, so I'll try not to breathe on you. I saw my breakfast twice this morning, so if I suddenly turn a darkish shade of yellow, and my lips begin trembling, don't panic, just step to the side and try to keep my shirttail out of it. My head, too, is pounding just for fun. Not even the three hundred Advil I took this morning is making a dent. I tend to exaggerate for effect. That's another one of my quirks that bothers Ruby. But if I said I took a couple of Advil, it would downplay the magnitude of my headache and drastically reduce sympathy. Ruby used to get migraines when she was younger, but they stopped once we got married. You'd think that that would work in my favor, but she explained that her migraine had simply taken human form.

But I have good news! That letter I wrote for my friend Charlie seems to be working. He has sent word that they have discontinued the chicken noodle soup. Of course, it was never about the soup, but what was in the soup, but at least they're addressing it. There's also a rumor going around that they're thinking about painting. You see? Progress. You can't sit by and wait for things to happen. Like Shakespeare said, "Once more to the breach, dear friend!"

Speaking of that great writer, there used to be a resident, now sadly deceased, who used to quote Shakespeare incessantly…Hello! Over here please! I see that your interest is waning, but you must hang in there. It is a delightful story, I assure you, and the telling of it will do wonders for my headache. So, in the name of human decency, please turn your attention away from the raccoon fight and…Thank you. I promise to make it worth your while.

So, like I was saying—please! The raccoon is a testy species. Their tempers flare up all the time. I'm sure if you wait long enough, you can catch another bout, whereas I may drop dead of a headache and you would never hear my story…

Okay then. So, this man thought he was entitled to Shakespeare's persona simply because his name happened to be Willie. I don't know what it is about Shakespeare's work that makes it so susceptible to bad imitation, but it seems like every time you turn around, someone is standing erect, looking out at a distant horizon, and saying, "But say, I prithee, is he coming home?" You can see how this would become tiresome.

It seems to me that if you're going to quote someone, you should at least take care to get the words right. Willie, however, was not interested in accuracy, so he'd say things like, "My eyes dripith tears of sorrow," if the gravy in the restaurant was running low. Or he'd tack on, "Kind person!" to the end of every sentence, which isn't even Shakespearean except in the delivery. But his favorite thing to do was to place a hand on your shoulder—please! Do you want me to continue the story or not? Are you paying attention? What is so special about a couple of screaming raccoons? Do they quote Shakespeare? Please, we are nearing the end and you are throwing my rhythm off completely.

Like I was saying, he would put his hand on your shoulder, tilt his head slightly, and say with a little smile, "Oh, the pits our conquerors dig to entrap us, dear friend." Absolutely maddening stuff that I'm sure had Shakespeare tugging at his death cloth. I too am guilty of stealing one of Shakespeare's lines. After one particularly nauseating performance, I strode up to Willie, and, in a voice inspired by the great stage performers of antiquity, said, "Told by an idiot, full of sound and fury!" He winced but quickly recovered and launched into a retelling of a dream he had had where Christopher Marlowe and Shakespeare wrestled each other in matching underwear—oh, for god's sake! I give up. You have entirely killed the punch line. Are you really more interested in the damn raccoons?

Strange, though I'll admit, how that one is up and running at us on hind legs.

Ms. Fisher

Dearest Laverne:

The gravy is runny today. I really hate that. The new cook is cute as a button but completely without talent. Maybe he's just nervous. Amato scares everyone. He doesn't scare me, though. If something isn't up to snuff, I'll tell him. The rolls are good. Not hard like they were last week. I think someone heated them up a bit too long. You know how that goes. Nuke them and they turn to stone.

My back is killing me. I had a dream that Art leapt on my back like a monkey and tried stabbing me with a butter knife. I must have been thrashing around. It feels like I threw my back out. Just one more reason to hate him, I guess. I haven't seen him today. I asked Holy Moses if he saw any trolls prowling around and he answered by asking me if I had any Doritos. That's the thing with Holy: big as a house and scary as heck if you don't know him, but Charlie Manson and his whole family could come parading through here and he'd give them your room key for a slice of sharp cheddar.

I guess I'll have to skip weight training today. Do you have weights at Sunny Grove? I didn't like them at first, but now I'm a regular Hercules. Me and some of the other women in my group are having shirts made that read Her-cules. Clever, I know.

I was against doing weights at first because Jennifer dated a boy in high school named Trent who lifted weights and drank milk all day long, and he had muscles that extended from his ear lobes clear out almost to his shoulders. Silliest thing I ever saw. What exactly are those muscles good for? I asked him, and you know what he said? "Can I have some more milk?" I told that story to Kelly and she was horrified. She has a problem with dairy. Anyway, I told Kelly that I didn't want to do weights because I didn't want to end up looking like Trent, which she thought was hysterical. "You need two things to get bulky, Fisher: Testosterone and lots and lots of food," she said. "And you're not a big eater." Ha, ha.

Brad, Kelly's boyfriend, is a bodybuilder. That's how he makes a living, if you can believe that. Don't ask me how. He's like Holy Moses: scary as all get out, but sweet. He wears this green workout number so everyone calls him the Jolly Green Giant. The amount of weight that man can lift is obscene. All us women huddle in little groups and try to act like we're not staring. It's hard not to. And what's funny, is that the men do the same thing. It got to be so bad that Kelly started restricting his visits because she doesn't like distractions in the gym. Now when Brad shows up everyone stops and treats him like a carnival side show because who knows when he'll be back.

Kelly's a real she-devil when it comes to exercise. Play the frail old lady card and she'll have you treading water wearing a weighted vest. She loves weights. She has me lifting them over my head and out to my sides and I do these things called lunges, which are just what you'd figure they'd be, but I call them loony lunges because that's what you have to be to go out of your way to do them. We also jump. We stand there, bend down and then jump as high as we can. I thought she was crazy the first time she suggested it, but Kelly has a way of suggesting that if you don't do what she says she'll pick out something much, much harder, so I did it, and it's actually kind of fun, if you're wearing the right sort of shoes.

Your only true friend,

B. A. Fisher

From the Archives
The Last Stop Bulletin

The Weather Front

Three guesses.

Upcoming Events

As much as we hate admitting when we are wrong, we owe Ms. Crocker an apology. What everyone swore—ourselves included—was a black bear, turned out to be a Newfoundland who stepped over his owner's fence and went down to the river to look for tadpoles. So I guess we're safe for now, though the coyotes seem to be getting louder.

Once again we have Holy Moses to thank. He spotted her down by the river and went down to investigate. They had some heated words, but came to an agreement before the fur started flying. All of this Harry witnessed as he ran towards them with an ax handle to see what all the commotion was about. Anyway, her name is Violet and she's nearly as big as our boy. She lives on the other side of the river in that Acres Green subdivision that has so thoroughly destroyed our view. Harry found her owners, Gloria and Todd, scouring the neighborhood. It never occurred to them that a water dog would go towards water, but they're young so we'll let it go.

For those of you scratching your heads wondering what the Upcoming Event is, hold your horses, we're getting to it. The short of it is that Violet and Holy spent the afternoon together while Gloria and Todd replaced their four-foot split-rail fence with a six-foot privacy, and are now inseparable. So Gloria and Violet will be spending Saturday afternoon with us. We know how god awfully sweet all of this is, but try to contain yourselves. We have had the pleasure of meeting Violet and she is a doll, but who knows how she'll react if seventy-eight of you rush her at the same time. Give her some space. She'll be here all afternoon, so everyone will get a chance to introduce themselves. The unknown, of course, is Holy. We all know how possessive he gets about certain things, so until we know how he's going to react, watch each other's backs.

You Ought to Know

And the shout went up, "Ms. Verney is back!" and it was true. She only asks that you try not to stare at the peeling skin just below her temples. But she has chucked the wig, and rumor has it she will be back in Beauty Inc. this weekend to get her hair done, which she says has come in kind of patchy. Hairdryers be damned! It takes more than a hot, blue flame to keep our girl down. And if that isn't enough, she has decided to be the first to go under the scissors with our new volunteer, Katelyn, who has a reputation of shakiness.

And speaking of Katelyn…some of us were thinking how interesting it is that Katelyn and Nathan are the same age, and how interesting it would be if they happened to bump into each other. It would also be interesting if they fell in love, got married and had lots of beautiful babies, but we're getting ahead of ourselves. We're big believers in letting love happen naturally, but it wouldn't hurt all you chatterboxes to put in a good word for Nathan. Besides, love is in the air; just ask Holy Moses.

As for all you old hell-hounds, be advised: Katelyn is cute, but much, much too young for you, so no gawking at her while she's cutting hair. She is very shy, and we don't want her distracted at some crucial moment. Behave.

The Hot Seat

Okay, Ms. Crocker. Just because we goofed up on the bear thing, doesn't mean you're off the hook. We've noticed that the herds have thinned out some, but we must remind you that bits of bread are just as unacceptable as nuts. It was never about the nuts, Ms. Crocker. Besides, we read somewhere that skunks like bread, so, by all means, continue. Oh, and don't think we don't see you out there late at night trying to lure them in by hand. Silly old girl, you're not fooling anyone.

The Suggestion Box

You have spoken and we have listened, but there is really no need for sarcasm. We are aware of what century it is, but we really had no idea how much faster DSL is than Dial Up. So excuse us if we thought the upgrade was an unnecessary expenditure. Excuse us for putting money into things like food and safe transportation. So now all of you can stop worrying about dying before your page loads like many of you suggested you might. But yes, we grudgingly admit, the difference is striking, so give yourselves a big round of applause. But don't clap too long. If you weren't being coached by your grandchildren, you would be, to quote Al Pacino, "In the dark here!" just as much as we are.

Holy Moses!

Violet tops the Holy Moses news today, but there is one other thing we thought we should bring up. Some of you may have noticed Holy's new nightly ritual where one minute he's sleeping peacefully, and the next he's tearing out the nearest exit where he pounces on something only he can see, roughs it up a bit, then returns inside and falls back asleep. The vet seems to think he's just exercising his creativity by making up suspense stories and then acting them out. Why doesn't this surprise us?

CASSANDRA

How are you this morning? Need anything? How about a bat to beat my ex boyfriend with? Sorry. I don't get really angry very often, but when I do I tend to flip out so if you want me to leave…

Vernon sent me flowers this morning. And that's not the worst of it. When he called Beverly to make sure they got here, she said his voice was quivering. He's got Beverly wrapped around his little finger. All she kept saying was, "It's so sweet," over and over again until I wanted to shake her.

I fell for the crying thing the first time I kicked him out. Funny how fast those little tears dried up after I agreed to let him move back in. And now he's using it on Beverly, who he doesn't even know. No, I will not let him use my apartment as a hash house. No, I will not let his stupid friends sleep on the couch when their girlfriends have a moment of clarity and throw them out. No, I will not listen to his drug-induced ramblings about how he's going to better himself and start going to night school.

You know what he got me for Valentine's Day every year for six years? A flipping teddy bear. Not a new, cute, clean teddy bear, but one he dug out of the bargain bin at the thrift store. The ones that have three generations of baby drool stuck to them. And who gets a grown woman a freaking teddy bear anyway? Did he think I was going to push it around in a little stroller? All it did was grin at me and remind me of what a cruddy boyfriend I had.

You know why I'm so mad? Because the first thing I said when I saw the flowers was, "Oh, how sweet." I actually said that. I throw up a little every time I think about it. But who doesn't like getting flowers? Of course, then I remembered that this was the same man that had once stolen a lawn mower and wheeled it down to the local pawn shop. Who does that? This little old guy left it idling in his yard while he went inside to get water or something, and Vernon, never one to miss an opportunity to be both ridiculous and a jerk, propelled it the seventeen blocks to the pawn shop.

Six freaking years I put up with him. Why would I want to go back to that? And even if he is trying to change, which I seriously doubt, we have nothing in common. You know what I do when I get home? I fix dinner, I take a long, hot bath, I get into my pajamas, I watch *CSI* with a glass of wine, and then I play my keyboard until my fingers cramp up, and you know what? That's exactly how I like it. I have no interest in narcotics, stealing, or hitting people in authority, and I know nothing about the prison system, except what I learned from watching *The Shawshank Redemption*. What in the world would we talk about? Certainly not Beethoven; certainly not Mozart. He'd probably watch *CSI* with me, but only because it would give him ideas.

And what's he going to do for a job? Who's going to hire him? He has no skills. If he thinks I'm going to let him sit on my couch all day eating potato chips and clipping job ads from the classifieds that he couldn't get in two thousand years, even if he didn't have a prison record, he's as dumb as I think he is.

And you know what kills me? It's not even me he wants. All he wants is a place to live and someone to take care of him. That way he doesn't have to do anything for the rest of his stupid life…

So, you never answered me. How are you this morning?

ASTER

Last night I had a dream that Ruby and Byron were running in the Race for the Cure, and I was there on the sidelines, swigging Jamison and lunging at them with a stick as they went by. It's funny how old wounds stay with you.

Here, I brought you these. I must apologize for my short temper the other day. I wasn't myself. I must also apologize for the close call with the raccoon. I had no idea they were that fast. I'm just thankful the doorknob was out of his reach.

If you don't like chocolate-covered cherries you can give them to someone or toss them in the waist basket, I just ask that you wait until after I've left to do so. I'm feeling better today. I woke up this morning craving spaghetti and meatballs, which is a sure sign of recovery.

I even did my prescribed thirty minutes on the stationary bike. It's easier now. One of the things that came out of the Ruby and Byron affair was that it forced me to take a close look at my bulging midsection. Intellectually, I could do figure eights around our friend Byron, but his physical conditioning, while not making up for the fact that he had—and still has unless he's started taking correspondence courses—the mental capacity of a slow third grader, was far superior to my own.

Gym had always been my weakest subject in school, so when it came time to try to match Byron physically, I sat down with Kelly to discuss what I needed to do. I had some experience with exercise after my doctor produced some startling cholesterol numbers and I made the mistake of trying to impress Kelly by telling her about my old regimen of pushups and sit-ups and jumping jacks. I even went so far as to brag about how I had worked up to doing fifty of each. What I neglected to tell her was that these were not done all at the same time, or even on the same day, but rather accomplished in sets of two or three over the course of several weeks.

I was hoping she'd say, "Great, do that," so I could go back to one of each every other day and think I was accomplishing something, but what she said was, "Jumping jacks? What are you a little girl? Come see me when you're serious." Had she known how unstable I was at the time, she might have tried a more sensitive approach. I was already feeling physically inadequate without being likened to a small child. But looking back, it probably wouldn't have mattered; sensitivity is not something she's overflowing with.

I've always suffered from overconfidence. It's been one of my major downfalls. That day when I got home from the doctor's office with my new workout program, I was so sure of my abilities that I immediately dropped down to the floor to do a quick set of five pushups just to get things moving. I figured that the required ten of each movement was preposterously low for a man of my means, so I quickly changed the number to fifty, but after getting down on the floor and realizing that I couldn't even hold my back straight, let alone push myself up and down, I assumed that I had misunderstood the time frame for the exercises. It never once occurred to me that maybe I was as out of shape as everyone said I was.

This same sort of thing happened the first time I went skiing with near fatal results. I figured I'd hit a blue run to get the blood circulating before tackling the black diamond. I didn't bother learning how to turn and I thought the poles were for beginners so I ditched them in the trees and started down in more or less a straight line. I heard Ruby's distant voice yelling, "Go down! Go down!" which I took to mean, "Go down the hill! Go down the hill!" which I did at roughly four-hundred and eighty miles an hour. After barreling through a patch of young aspen trees, breaking through the fence barrier and mowing down a family of eight waiting for the chairlift, I came to a rolling stop at the entrance to the ski shop, where I threw the obviously defective skis through the threshold and told the man working there that he would hear from my lawyer.

Oh, I almost forgot to tell you. You know who I got a call from last night? Val Kilmeir. Ever since the "incident" we've struck up a casual friendship. Of course he's under the impression that we share an interest in stamp collecting, which I know nothing about and have no real desire to learn, but I have a talent for shifting the topic of conversation when it gets too technical—do you think worms have eyeballs? You see? Easy as pie.

Ms. Fisher

Dearest Laverne:

    This is how my day started. I was out on the patio looking at a bunch of dirt that had blown all over the place, mucking up my sitting area. I usually keep a broom propped up against the wall next to the planters for just such an occasion, but it wasn't there. Mr. Jenson was out in the courtyard doing stretches and was in a perfect position to see if anyone had snatched it, so I called out to him, "Mr. Jenson, have you seen my broom?"

And he yelled back, "Where'd you park it?"

Everyone's a comedian these days.

Do you think I'm losing my edge? Do you think age is softening me? I don't normally suffer smart alecks. Normally if someone made a crack like that I'd borrow a broom and beat them with it. But I didn't. I even told him he was funny, which shocked him just as much as it shocked me. I've built a reputation around here based on fear and intimidation. What if word gets out and everyone starts thinking they can get away with cracks like that?

I bring all this up because there was this ugly, little man on Oprah the other day and he was talking about anger and guilt and all the other crap we carry around with us, and one thing he kept saying was that it takes a lot more energy to be angry than it does to be happy. Is this true? You're one of the happy ones. I've been really tired lately. I don't want to think that it's because I'm angry most of the time, but Oprah seemed to agree with him and she's right about most things.

But it's not like I'm cruel. Mean-ish, maybe. I don't call people names or point unless it's justified. The way I see it, I keep things in balance. if everyone was happy, no one would know it because they wouldn't have anything to compare it to. Maybe I'll write a letter to Oprah and she can chew on that one awhile.

Mary Stuart should have been on Oprah. They would have gotten along famously. Mary used to always say things like, "Never worry about the things you can't control," which is a lot easier said than done, but we'd probably all live a lot longer if we could manage it. She was always saying things like that, and she was one of the few that could actually pull it off. And she was nice—my god that woman was nice! You could call her every name in the book and she'd offer you a muffin.

But if you think I'm miserable, you should see the new guy across the hall. You'll appreciate this. His name is Harold or something and he walks like the weight of the whole world is smashing down on him. And he won't look you in the eye unless you say something to him, which I made the mistake of doing. I passed him on my way to breakfast this morning, looking gloomy as ever, and you know how much I like sarcasm, so I say, "Morning chipper!" and he launches into this tirade about how his hair is falling out and how his ears hurt and how his eyesight is going and how he can't read the labels on the whole slew of pills he's taking, and how once he starts taking his pills, he gets to a point where he can't remember which ones he's taken and which ones he hasn't so he doesn't take any more, so now he figures he's dying of something but he has no way of know what of because he doesn't know which pills he's not taking. Jesus. And then his feet hurt, and he can't eat broccoli… on and on and on, so I steered this little bundle of joy to the office Kelly keeps next to the pool, shoved him in and slammed the door behind him. The only thing Kelly dislikes more than mayonnaise is complainers, and I once saw her throw a jar of mayonnaise clear across the Fitness Center when she caught Diego using it as dip for his carrot sticks.

I'm not sure what she did to him, but I saw him a couple of hours later looking disheveled and he had the blank stare of someone just back from a near death experience.

Your only true friend,

B. A. Fisher

From the Archives
The Last Stop Bulletin

The Weather Front

Well, we hate to say it, but we might be in for a little too much of a good thing. Uncle Heat Wave is high tailing it out of town to make room for his smelly, foul-mouthed cousin, Captain Cold N. Dreary, and he's known for his extended stays. But to Uncle Heat Wave we must say, "Good riddance! You have burned us. You have dehydrated us. You have brought our faithful maintenance man to the brink, and you have killed everything green and pretty with your evil rays, so be gone! Come back when you learn moderation."

Okay, now that we've gotten that out of our system, it's going to be wet, bleak and dismal, or pleasantly cool and cozy, however you wish to look at it for the next couple days, so dust off the sweaters and raincoats. You might want to take this opportunity to crack open that book you've been meaning to read or clean out the pantry…we're just throwing out ideas.

Upcoming Events

Sorry guys, but we're going to have to deny your Friday night movie request. We realize that a lot of effort went into getting seventy-eight percent of the male residents to vote, but *Basic Instinct* will not be befouling our theater while any of us are still alive. We found your argument over the film's merits shallow and laughable, particularly the gushing over the films groundbreaking cinematography. So, in the words of Bugs Bunny, "For shame, doc!" and just for that, we're ordering the extended version of *The Bridges of Madison County*.

You Ought to Know

We have been banging our heads against the wall all morning and have come to the conclusion that as far as we're concerned there is absolutely nothing You Ought to Know other than what you already know from reading this bulletin. We'll try again tomorrow, but we make no promises.

The Hot Seat

If you don't mind Ms. Zuckerman, go ahead and squeeze in next to Ms. Crocker in The Hot Seat. We know all about your recent run-ins with "that damn squirrel," but you two are just going to have to find a way to live with each other, and threatening Ms. Crocker isn't going to help things. We know, it was Ms. Crocker, not you, who invited "that damned squirrel," but it wasn't as though she whispered (at least we don't think) in his little ear to attack you every time you step foot outside. So please no more confrontations. There is a remote possibility that he would have shown up without Ms. Crocker tempting him with goodies, and since no one speaks squirrel, we are going to have to dismiss the charges.

However, Ms. Crocker, the case concerning the Mountain Goats and the family of Snow Leopards who wandered in from the high mountains of Central Asia, is still very much on the docket. So, Ms. Zuckerman, instead of Googling (aren't we high tech!) "Killing squirrels in your spare time," like a number of residents reportedly saw you doing, perhaps you should try to be friends with the little rodent.

The Suggestion Box

You have spoken and we have listened, and in turn, we have spoken to Randy about playing Pantera (thank you, Bettie, for writing down the name of the band; success is in the details) while driving the transport van, and, though we can't be certain, we think he listened. We are aware that insane music like that makes him drive much faster than is safe, and many of you became car sick. One other thing: that horrible screeching noise you all mistook for the wheels falling off was actually just the power steering. Apparently it gets cranky when it's thirsty.

Holy Moses!

Holy has had a busy week, and it seems to be catching up with him. It doesn't happen very often, but our boy is moody. He won't eat, not even cheese. Randy took him to see Dr. Floyd this morning, but despite suggesting that Holy lose a few pounds, he gave him a clean bill of health. If you have any ideas, let us know. We let him watch *Turner and Hootch* on the big screen, but not even that helped. Violet will be here later this afternoon, so maybe she can cheer him up. In the mean time, try not to get in his way.

CASSANDRA

So get this: I'm sitting at home playing *Chopsticks*—I know horrible, right?—but it's one of the few things I can play all the way through, and I'm kind of in a zone because it's late and I'm watching this woman modeling pantyhose on the shopping network and I don't realize that I've got the volume on my keyboard way up because I'm mesmerized by this woman's feet. Anyway, I start hearing this banging noise, but it doesn't faze me because someone is always banging on something in my complex, so I don't realize that it's actually a guy who just moved in beneath me and he's pounding on the ceiling trying to get me to shut up. But I'm tired so I figure he's hanging a picture or something so I start stomping on the floor because now he's the one annoying me. And I'm still stomping when he starts pounding on my door. I'm mad because I'm tired and now my practicing has been disrupted, so I throw open the door—which I shouldn't have done because I was alone and it might have been a serial killer, or worse, Vernon—and I'm in my pajamas and I had let my hair air dry when I got out of the shower so it's sticking up and matted in weird places, and this guy is standing there all red-faced and glaring and breathing heavy and I say, "Yes," and he sighs really long and says, "Please tell me you know other songs," and I start cracking up because it dawns on me that I've been playing *Chopsticks*, by far the most annoying song every written outside of *Twinkle*, over and over and over again for like two hours, and this poor guy is down there pulling his hair out trying to figure out how to get out of his lease, so I told him, "I'm soooo sorry," and that I'm crazy and a Mozart nut and his face turned its natural color, which is actually pretty pale—not surprising, though, since he's a redhead named Eric—I know, I know, his name has nothing to do with his complexion, I just figured at some point you'd ask me his name so I threw it in there. His name isn't important, though, because he's not my type, but he does know who Mozart is—or was—and he told me about a movie called *Amadeus,* which is all about his life—Mozart's not Eric's—and won a bazillion awards. I'm going to watch it, but not with him because he has freckles and his name is Eric, which I have a real problem with because the second most traumatic experience in my life, after Lucinda what's-her-name shoving paste up my nose, concerned a little redheaded monster named Eric who put a wad of chewing gum— Big League chewing gum, like the whole pouch of it—in my hair and my mom had to use extra crunchy peanut butter to get it out because it was the only kind we had and the whole experience has given me nightmares ever since because the peanut butter looked and felt like brains, so Eric, even though he likes Mozart, which counts for a lot, doesn't have a shot, poor guy, unless Vernon shows up and I have to scream for help and he comes and saves my life or something, obligating me to go out with him, but I don't see that happening because along with being a redhead and having a bad name, he has the build of someone who just staggered out of the woods after living on berries for three months and Vernon, despite being horrible and ugly in every other way, has muscles from here to wherever and Eric wouldn't stand a chance even if he had an identical twin to help him—God I've got a headache. I tried this new drink this morning called *Zing!* but as far as I can tell, it doesn't do anything at all but give you a headache. Weird.

ASTER

Kelly almost killed me again. Unintentional, I think. The truth is I think I exasperate her. She's never been my biggest fan. I'm stubborn. I know this about myself. I have very strong opinions, even on things I don't know much about. I sometimes speak without thinking. That was ultimately my downfall, I think, with Ruby, along with other things. I haven't always been the easiest person to live with. I'm afraid I spent a lot of my time exasperating her, too.

The incident was remarkable similar to one that happened the day of my first real workout, so I will relate that one since it advances our story and it will give you some idea about what happened this morning. I was wearing my new yellow sweatpants and sweatbands. I also had a towel, three candy bars for energy, two bottles of water, and a heart rate alarm system that would shriek if my heart rate was elevated above 80bpm. Perhaps all of this got us off to a bad start.

She was showing me proper technique on the bench press. I told her several times that the exercise seemed to be inferior to my pushup routine. Why would you want to go to all the trouble of trying to balance a ridiculously long bar when you can push yourself up from the floor without all the hassle?

Kelly, too, is very opinionated, especially on things related to health and fitness, so she didn't waste any time pointing out that unlike my beloved pushups, you can change the weight and therefore the resistance. This made sense, but then it dawned on me that one could increase the number of repetitions just as easily, and again without all the hassle of loading and unloading the weight. She was not amused and informed me that "hassling" me was exactly what she was after. This struck me as uncalled for, but it did nothing to dissuade me. I then voiced my concern with having such a heavy load teetering over me, waiting for my grip to give out so it could come down and crush me. I tend to get excited when I think I'm winning an argument, and this last bit came out more heated than I intended.

Kelly's eyes flashed, and, after uttering a short, exasperated laugh, she launched into a tirade for the ages. I didn't catch all of it because her voice rose to such a volume that words became distorted and demon-like. I did catch something about overloading the pectoral muscles and something about stabilizer muscles, but the rest was a garbled mess of obscenities.

After a few minutes she regained her composure and told me simply that if I knew what was good for me, I'd stop complaining and get under the damn bar.

I thought it best to submit. She had demonstrated through her body language that she was not above using violence if necessary to get her point across. So I did what I was told and got under the damn bar, which must have been loaded with several hundred pounds because I could barely lift it off the rack. I slowly lowered it to my chest and found, not surprisingly, that no matter how hard I pushed, no matter how much I flopped around on the bench, I couldn't budge the bar even a little. I tried to get Kelly's attention by stomping my left foot, but she was busy discussing the finer points of interval training with Beth Alderman who was on the station directly behind us. By this time, the bar had worked its way down to the base of my throat, and there it sat, toying with me.

I tried once more to get her attention, this time by stomping both feet, one after the other. I had too much pride to scream or cry, both of which seemed appropriate. And then Kelly, without looking, reached down with two fingers and lifted the bar off my neck and set it back in the rack.

Now, having been so close to death with nothing noble to show for it, I was understandably upset and threw caution to the wind. I pointed and yelled that I could have been killed, showering her with little drops of spittle. I paced and frothed and shook my finger at her...and all for nothing. You know what she said when I had finished? She said, "Good, bring that intensity with you next time, and maybe we can put some actual weight on the bar."

Ms. Fisher

Dearest Laverne:
 Please look at the enclosed picture before reading further...
Now, is that or is that not the Deadly Nightshade? It was in front of my
door this morning, and before I thought better about it, I brought it in
and smelled it and put it in one of my best vases, and now I'm probably
dying. Look it up if you don't believe me. It's like the Venus Flytrap. It
droops over and plays dead and lures you in with its pretty purple and
yellows until you get close enough, and then WHAM! it poisons you and
before you know it you start convulsing, your eyes dilate and you flop
over dead. And it does all of this for its own amusement.

So if this letter ends abruptly, you'll know what happened. I have
left a note just in case, which reads, "HE DID IT!" with a little arrow
pointing to a picture of Art. I've also left instructions to forward this
letter to you as my final communication.

I don't mean to concern you but my left arm is going numb.

It must be Art. That explains the cookies, too. I told you he was
sneaking around. Instead of jumping out of the bushes with a kitchen
knife like a proper serial killer, he sends me an assassin plant.

Maybe I'm being paranoid, but I've recruited the twins, Mandy M
and Sandy D to keep an eye out for me. I don't think I've told you
about them. If you can tell them apart, I'll make you a bologna sandwich.
They've been here over a year and I still have no idea which one is which.
You can start a story with one of them and pick up where you left off the
next day with the other one and never know it because they never let on.

They nod and smile and give you the feeling that *Rod Serling* is going to jump out of the closet.

It's getting really hot in here, and one of the yellow bulbs just drooped over. Maybe it's just my imagination.

Mandy and Sandy are nature girls. They wear matching flannel shirts every day, even in August when it's a hundred degrees. They're up every morning at five-thirty. I know this because their room is next to mine, and I hear them giggling every morning at the same time. The walls aren't even thin, that's how loud they're laughing. I'm going to find out what's so funny, if I don't die first. I tried asking them one time and they fell into each other's arms and said, "Oh, we couldn't tell you that!" It's driving me mad.

Anyway, they're out the door and walking the trails by sun up and they're not back until mid morning. They usually wander into the restaurant just about the time I'm finishing my hash browns, and sit down to a plate of gravy covered everything. They even put it on vegetables. Kelly can't even get to them because for all of their atrocious eating habits, they're both fit like you've never seen. I saw one of them one time—don't ask me which one—in a t-shirt and she had veins in her arms and everything. It must be all the walking.

Anyway, I gave them a picture of Art so they can be on the lookout. If he's out there lurking around in the woods, they'll know about it. You can't hide from the twins. They ha—

From the Archives
The Last Stop Bulletin

The Weather Front

We hope you found something good to read, because today is more of the same, only colder and with more driving rain. If you find yourself sulking, think about Harry. Because he can't mow, he has to start working on the annual to-do list provided by the Board, chalk full of things like air vent cleaning and removing scuff marks in the lobby by hand. If you need anything fixed in your rooms, don't hesitate to ask. Despite the to-do list, he seems to be highly approachable; he even outfitted Holy with a tool belt. We are of the opinion that it is impossible to be snippy when in the presence of Holy Moses wearing a tool belt.

Upcoming Events

You may have noticed that despite all the painters hanging around, not much painting is getting done, so starting tomorrow they are being replaced by The Epstein Brothers Painting Crew, all nine of them. It's no secret that they smoke marijuana, but they work quickly, which is a weird sort of oxymoron. With all the news of painting, some of you have expressed interest in the color scheme, so here it is: Bungle house Blue. Rembrandt Ruby for the trim. All the doors will be Vogue Green, and if you don't like it, don't come running to us, take it up with the Board. Rest assured you will get no response from them. Because of the crew's moderate drug use, Harry will be keeping a close eye on them. Harry doesn't like potheads.

You Ought to Know

We have an update on Barb's plan to leave us. Mr. Henley overheard her speaking to someone on the phone about having second thoughts. Keep it up! We've got her on the ropes. Remember, the idea is that the whole facility will come crashing down if she leaves. Body shot, body shot, knock her out!

The Hot Seat

Well, it had to happen sooner or later. For all the punishment we dish out, there was bound to be an occasion when we had no choice but to place ourselves in The Hot Seat. We owe Ms. Zuckerman an apology. We had no idea that squirrels were so against making friends with humans. It was like something from *When Animals Attack*. No tape exists so we'll just have to rehash the story of the Damn Squirrel launching himself off the birdbath and into Ms. Zuckerman's hair around the campfire. Perhaps Ms. Zuckerman will provide the soundtrack.

The damage done was mostly emotional, but she did suffer some deep scratches about her cheek and neck, so again we apologize. We also apologize for Ernie going after the squirrel with a garden rake while it was still attached to Ms. Zuckerman's head. In the end, however, we must thank him, because it did stop the mauling.

The Suggestion Box

Harry has spoken and we have listened. Due to the overwhelming outcry over the stamina stairs closing, Harry has submitted plans to build a safer set. We only got a peek at the plans, but they appear to be just as high as the originals, but free-standing and with safety slides running along the sides in case you get stuck. That is all we know, but we feel pretty confident that the steps themselves will be made of something more forgiving than wood. Don't start jumping for joy just yet. The plan has yet to be approved.

Holy Moses!

Hurray for Violet! The mysterious ailment afflicting Holy Moses has been solved. No sooner than the big girl walked in, our boy was up and showing off how fast he could run and jump. What a good girl she is. She even pretended not to notice when Holy wiped out after taking a corner too sharply. According to Gloria, Violet hasn't been herself lately either, and has been chewing on their new fence. So, in the interest of new fences and good karma, Gloria will be dropping Violet off every morning on her way to work and picking her up on her way home. We just wish Mary Stuart could be here to see her favorite boy happily, hopelessly in love.

CASSANDRA

Do you think I'm getting fat? I've gained five pounds since last week and I can't find it. It's here somewhere. It's probably waiting to pop up when I least expect it. I'll probably wake up tomorrow with two asses. I told Kelly I wanted to get down to 125lbs and she told me to throw away my scale. "What if you get down to 125lbs and your ass is still flabby?" she said. "Concentrate on the flab, not the scale." I don't know if she thinks my ass is flabby or if she was just using an example. So now I've been staring at my ass all morning. I've seen it from every possible angle, and I don't think its "flabby" per se, but the potential is definitely there so I'm borderline freaking out.

Mary Stuart used to go around asking people if her ass was flabby just to make us laugh. She didn't say ass, though, she said butt or can. She was one of those people you assumed would live forever. My luck Vernon will live forever. Do you see what he's doing to me? I'm turning into one of those people who say, "That's just my luck." I don't want to be one of those people. I've always been a big fan of the Brightside, but now every time I try to look on the Brightside, Vernon's dumb head pops up like a jack-in-the-box. And I've developed a really bad mouth lately. The words that come out of my mouth sometimes, I don't know. They're a lot worse than ass, I'll tell you that. And the word Vernon is usually somewhere in the sentence. You know what this means, right? We have to come up with a way to keep him in prison. I'm thinking about seeing if the lawnmower guy would be willing to press charges. I don't know what the statute of limitations is on stealing lawnmowers, but it might be worth a shot.

I tried to return the flowers, by the way, but the mailman wouldn't take them. Maybe I'll chop them up into little tiny pieces and send them in an envelope. Beverly is no help at all. I know they talk on the phone. She might be encouraging him for all I know. I guess she'll just have to be the one to console him when he shows up here and I tell him to go drown himself.

And if Vernon isn't enough, now I've got Eric to deal with, too. I told you about Eric, right? Red hair, freckles, likes Mozart. Well, he's really very nice…too nice…the kind of nice that makes your mouth fill up with saliva. I shouldn't say that, but now that he knows I like Mozart, he keeps leaving little gifts outside my door. I know it's him because I saw him streaking down the hall when I came home the other night. And, besides, who else knows I like Mozart? So first it was a Mozart keychain, which was kind of nice; then it was a little doll wearing an I Love Mozart shirt, which was kind of creepy, and this morning I found a little figurine that's supposed to be Mozart but looks like Mr. Hyde and he's holding a little note that says, "I've just bought a Sony. Maybe we can practice together??????" So now I'm a prisoner in my own home. How am I supposed to tell him that my learning the piano and listening to Mozart is a very personal thing and that I'd really rather not share it with someone who sneaks around late at night leaving gifts for people he hardly knows? See what I mean? Complain, complain, complain. You've got to help me find the Brightside again soon or I'll go crazy. You don't want a crazy Cassandra on your hands, believe me.

I know what you're thinking. I can see it in your eyes. You're thinking that Eric might be just what I need right now: a nice convenient boyfriend just in time for Vernon to get out of prison. It wouldn't work. Vernon would take one look at Eric and know something was up. And even if he did think that Eric and I were together, it wouldn't discourage him. Look how horrible you turned out to be: wanting to use and abuse poor little freckled Eric. You should be ashamed of yourself.

ASTER

Have you tried the potato skins? Amato has a bad habit of trying to get creative with everything, but these he usually leaves alone, and they're excellent. A few years ago he put sour cream and horse-radish in the eggs without telling anyone and it almost caused a riot. Not as bad as that French guy, Buckland, or whatever his name was, that used to stew moles and fry earwigs, but when you start tampering with the food, it's a slippery slope. Kind of like lying: before you know it you're robbing banks.

...It's funny how certain things and places bring memories flooding back. You see that booth over there by the door? That's where I finally found Ruby. She was there with a couple of her lady friends. The timing couldn't have been worse. It was the day after I started my workout sessions with Kelly. After the bench press incident, she felt so bad that she decided to torture me for the next half hour. It took every ounce of energy to roll out of bed the next morning. Everything hurt. My face, even, from grimacing, I imagine, even though the bar she had me using during the workout was made out of foam.

Now, I'm not a fan of physical comedy routines. The Three Stooges always struck me as annoying, but the series of events that happened when I sat down to my coffee would have made them proud. When I tried lifting my coffee cup to my lips, it came up short and dumped, steaming, all down the front of me, causing me to recoil and fall backwards out of my chair, smacking the back of my head on the counter. I then preformed a perfect midair barrel roll and landed face first on the linoleum. I am not usually prone to performances like this, you understand, and I'm not used to seeing the kitchen flooring that close up. I must have been dazed, because I decided to mosey on down to the restaurant instead of cooking my usual two eggs over easy. This by itself isn't so awful, but for some reason I felt that changing out of my coffee-stained shirt was just as unnecessary as finding my other shoe. Add to this my sore, shoeless foot dragging behind me and my hair matted with some unknown substance, and you will begin to understand the abject horror I felt upon seeing that my elusive wife had a front row seat to this performance.

This, you understand, was not at all how the confrontation scene was supposed to play out. I was supposed to be casually strolling down the hall in my blue slacks, my hair recently cut, my golf shirt pressed and sharp, whistling a show tune. I would come upon Ruby and Byron in some heated argument and stop just long enough to wish them good day and offer counseling. The upper hand is what I was after. Someone once said that the best revenge is living well, and it was obvious to one and all that I was doing anything but.

Things tend to escalate with me. It doesn't take much to get the ball rolling. I don't know if this phenomenon is common with other people, or if it is some disease of the mind reserved for a lucky few, but when things start heading dramatically in one direction or another, good or bad, I tend to do everything I can to get more of the same. The smart thing to do would have been to exit stage left, return to my room, clean myself up and return as though the homeless man they had seen few minutes prior was a figment of their imagination. But, alas, this is not my way. I thought it best to laugh hysterically and point, and approach them, and slide into the booth across from Ruby and snatch her bagel and begin eating it.

"There she is!" I said. "There's my girl." Marge and Phyllis, her lady friends, looked like they might suddenly attack me with their forks and butter knives, but Ruby's expression never changed

"I see you've been taking care of yourself," Ruby said.

"I have, thanks, glad you noticed. I had a slight mishap with my coffee this morning, but beyond that I'm shipshape. You know it's great to see you?" I was vaguely aware that I was talking really loud, and that the people around us were starting to stare.

Phyllis and Marge are textbook man-haters, and seeing me there at such an obvious disadvantage had them giddy. I was, to their way of thinking, everything that was wrong with the male species. They used to tolerate me because of Ruby, but now that ties had been severed, they were free to let loose on me.

Phyllis was the first to speak. "Perhaps you can help us, Aster," she said, "we've been sitting here with this crossword puzzle wracking our brains trying to come up with a five letter word for old, disheveled—"

"And annoying," Marge added. "It starts with an A."

"Any ideas," Phyllis said, and they both shook with inward laughter.

I normally don't' resort to name calling or insulting implications, but I asked them if they wouldn't mind retreating to their caves so I could speak to my wife.

"I thought your wife left you," Marge said.

"That's what I heard," Phyllis said.

To Ruby's credit, she wasn't participating. I tried smashing down the matted hair on the side of my head in an effort to seem cool and collected and then asked Ruby, "Where are you staying?" knowing full well the answer and preparing to hear it out loud.

"I'm staying with Lizzy—"

"Lies!" I yelled. Then I yelled it again because it sounded Shakespearean.

"Don't cause a scene—"

"Lies! Where is he?"

"Where is who?"

"Who, for god's sake?"

"Yes, Aster, the question is who?"

"Byron, Byron, Byron!" This got the attention of the whole restaurant, including Amato who poked his head out of the kitchen.

"Byron, Aster? Really?" She shook her head. "I'm not going to do this here. I'll be by the room later this afternoon to get the rest of my things. We can talk then. Just promise to put some clothes on and behave rationally."

"Lies!" I said again, but I agreed.

Ms. Fisher

Dearest Laverne:
    I know, dear, that was horrible. I'm not dead. I was never a good practical joker. I was feeling weird, but it was probably the cherry peppers I'd had earlier acting up. The embarrassing thing is that the plant isn't the Nightshade at all. It's not even the right colors. I don't know what I was thinking. I double checked a volume called *The Killers in the Backyard* and it's not in there. At least they're not plastic. Then I'd feel really dumb.

I have you to thank. I got your card and remembered it was my birthday and I checked the death plant and lo and behold there was a "happy birthday" sign jammed down in the pot. Just so you know, your card wasn't late, I was just so frazzled that I didn't go and get my mail. So my birthday came and went and I didn't even realize it. Not that that's such a bad thing. Who needs birthdays anymore? At this point it's like counting down the years you have left, and who needs that? To tell you the truth, if you asked me yesterday when I was born I'd have to stop and think about it for a minute. That's the way it should be. What is age? What is time? Everyone's going to die, no sense having your own personal doomsday clock running. Live your life, and then one day you'll get hit by a bus and hopefully you won't linger too long. And that's that. Put another quarter in the cosmos.

So you would logically think that the flowers were from my loving daughter, but you'd be wrong. She has never remembered my birthday. The closest she came was about five years ago when she asked me three weeks late, "Isn't your birthday sometime in the summer?"

It turns out that the flowers were from Ernie down the hall. There wasn't a card or anything with them, but Shirley, my Care Provider, said that she saw Ernie put them in front of my door and run away. I'm eighty years old—sorry, eighty-one years old—and someone has a crush on me, imagine that.

At first I thought it was very nice, but then, which is usually the case with me, I became angry. How on god's green earth am I supposed to know someone is interested in me if they don't even have the guts to put a card with their gift? I'm not a mind reader. I don't have time for secret admirers. If you want something, go get it for crying out loud. I don't like people that allude to things and I don't like assumptions and I don't like riddles.

So that's the annoying part about it. The somewhat creepy part is that he knew it was my birthday at all, considering that I didn't even know it was my birthday, which leads me to wonder what other things he knows about me. But what are you going to do? If he wants to stay up late at night researching me and my sketchy past, who am I to stop him?

So what do you think I should do with this little piece of information? I can't confront him. I'm not interested in seeing a grown man wet himself. Not that I'm saying that I would never have anything to do with a man like Ernie. I prefer my men to have a backbone, but perhaps he can develop one. He is cute, in a mousy sort of way. I'm not saying we're going to get married or anything, I'm just saying we may have dinner one night or something. Never say never. I don't know, though. We are talking about a man who eats his green beans with a spoon.

Your only true friend,

B. A. Fisher

From the Archives
The Last Stop Bulletin

The Weather Front

Due to recent events (see The Hot Seat) and the bleak weather we've been having we have discontinued the steak knives out of fear that you might turn them on yourselves or your peers. The butter knives will remain in play. If you manage to do any damage with those, we feel you should be rewarded for your efforts.

The wind will be whipping rain drops at fifty miles an hour later this afternoon, so we suggest you stay inside. We know, Ms. Patterson, those little ice darts sting worse than bees, that's why we're bringing it up.

Upcoming Events

Please welcome Julie Weaver to the team. Because Mary Stuart's condition isn't improving, and the doctors are not at all confident in her recovery, we have hired Julie as a temporary driver to ensure that everyone has a chance to visit Mary in the hospital. Julie will also be filling in when Randy goes on vacation next month. She has assured us that she will drive the posted speed limit and will only run from the police if pressed. That part of her life, she says, is mostly behind her.

You Ought to Know

No one is taking the recent weather change harder than Harry, who planted three hills of geraniums, twelve plots of roses, and sixteen new aspen trees outside the Fitness Center. If you listen, you can hear them throwing themselves against the side of the building. Last year Harry lost seven trees. The death toll this year looks like it could double and Harry is almost possessed. We have started soliciting funds to replace his coat, which was torn when it became entangled in the limbs of one of the trees he was trying to save. Please don't try to console him. He is unpredictable in times of stress, especially when the wind is blowing his hair into his eyes.

The Hot Seat

Whatever the circumstances surrounding our very own "Rumble in the Jungle" the other evening, we have no choice but to put all participants in The Hot Seat. Who started it we have no way of knowing since sides have been taken and witnesses aren't talking. What the argument was about we don't know, nor do we care much. The fact is that for sixty years we have prided ourselves on being a safe, happy place in which to retire. Everyone needs to release every now and then, but when the cops have been called and the paramedics have been rushed in, we must say, "You have gone too far!" There are plenty of ways to prove your superiority to your fellow residents without resorting to barroom tactics. So if you have a disagreement with someone, we urge you to use some sort of healthy competition to settle your dispute.

The Suggestion Box

Well, this is a first. You have either not spoken, or we have become both hard of hearing and blind. We triple checked The Suggestion Box, but still nothing. We take your silence as evidence that everything is perfect in every conceivable way, so we will be discontinuing The Suggestion Box...We just want to see if anyone actually reads this.

HOLY MOSES!

There must be something in the water. As most of you probably know, Violet's visit didn't go as expected, and now Holy Moses shares the distinction of having spilled blood on the premises. Who knew Holy Moses was so horny? We've never seen him like that. She tolerated most of it, but when he bit her neck, and tried to take her down, she let him have it. And we say, "Good for her!" Alas, Holy is now one ear short of a pair.

Before anyone starts fainting, it was only the top third of the ear and he's bandaged up and doing fine. We've got him laid up in Mary's suite with enough pain killers to put the whole facility to sleep. Two weeks from now, it will be like it never happened. And before any of you start harboring ill thoughts towards Violet, we should tell you that she rode with him to the vet and licked his mangled ear the whole way. What a nice girl! A lesser Violet would have relieved him of his other ear, too.

CASSANDRA

Kill me now. Have you ever agreed to something and then later—like three seconds later—felt like throwing yourself in front of a speeding train? Ms. Farley came up to me and went on this long speech about how Mr. Jenson's arthritis is worse than ever and how he won't be able to play the piano in the recital later this month. So she wants me to take his place. Do you know what this means? I have three weeks to muster up the courage to mangle one of my hands so I can't play. Can you imagine me in front of a room full of people? And if that isn't bad enough, she said that this would be a good warm up for Christmas, meaning I'm going to be playing in that, too. "Don't worry," she said. "I'm sure you'll be really good." I told her that saying "really good" about my piano playing is like saying "decorative dog turds" which she thought was hysterical, but missed my larger point. And just for fun, she warned me that the piano I'll be playing is really old and that the pedals sometimes stick and the bench is wobbly. Pedals? I've never even used pedals.

The only thing to do, I guess, is to first tell Ms. Farley that I agreed before thinking it through and that I can't play after all, thus breaking her heart, and then I need to find out whoever told her that I had taken up the piano and poison their lunch. I already know who did it. There are exactly two people in this building that know about it, and I know you wouldn't put me in that position. The other person is Beverly, whom I would kill if she wasn't so sweet and loveable. She means well, but she's currently ruining my life in multiple ways. I made the mistake of looking at one of her catalogs she keeps at her desk and there were keyboards in it and I asked—not so much her, just kind of thinking out loud—where you go to buy a cheap piano, and before I knew what was happening she was grabbing my hand and telling me how amazing I play even though, obviously, she has never heard me. You see? How can you be angry with someone like that? And I'll bet you everything I own that if I played for her right now and showed her just how awful I really am, she'd still say I was amazing. I'm going to have to talk to her, though. I just hope I don't make her cry.

Anyway, I can't go through with it. I told my mom about it and she fed me some nonsense about tackling the things that scare us, and "what doesn't kill you makes you stronger," which sounds good but I can't see how me passing out and falling backwards off the piano bench is going to make me stronger. I hate to do this to Ms. Farley. She's going to be crazy disappointed. She was really excited about it. Maybe I can find someone to fill in for me. I don't want to think about it anymore. If I do, I'm likely to be sick.

Okay, to drastically change the subject…I'm letting Eric take me out tonight—I know, I know, I said not in a million years. You don't have to remind me about the freckles and the chicken legs and the weird gifts and the pipe cleaners masquerading as arms. I know all that, but I've seen the worst the male population has to offer in Vernon, so how bad could he be? Maybe he's smart and funny, you never know. He's not into drugs or stealing lawnmowers, I know that, and maybe that's enough. How's that for standards? It's just that he's trying so hard. Anyway, it's just dinner. I'll be sure to give you all the gory details.

Oh, by the way, when your next exam is due, I might have to bring my trainee along with me, and I might have to actually let her touch you, which is scary because she might get distracted by a blue jay outside and accidentally shove the stethoscope up your nose…

ASTER

More good news on the Charlie front. The orange juice stains that usually accompany his letters were absent, which tells me that he has ditched the Sippy cup for something more appropriate for a man his age, and his handwriting borders on legible, which means he's no longer writing from the confines of his bed. But what's more surprising is that he is upbeat and chatty, two conditions you would sooner find in Attila the Hun. He says that the hooded form that usually sits on the edge of his bed forever checking his watch and shaking Charlie's foot is gone. And instead of spending up to twenty-three hours in bed, he is now up at six-thirty for eggs and biscuits, followed by a stroll down the newly painted Green Mile to the library where he's currently reading a riveting account of the settlement at Plymouth Rock before the pilgrims started sneaking off with the Indians' corn.

Isn't that wonderful? It is undeniable proof that human beings can change if they put their minds to it. It's all perspective. Give someone a little hope, a little support, show them a little fresh paint, green grass and sunshine, and feed them a good biscuit with real butter and, Poof, you have a whole new human being. I must be honest, however, that I wasn't sure if he was going to pull out of his slump. Once your pillow has become your constant companion, and you start ending all of your correspondence with, "If I'm dead tomorrow, you were a good friend," you've crossed a line that isn't easy to go back on. But I've learned to expect the unexpected. In this case, the unexpected was much for the better; in the case of Ruby returning to the room that day so we could "talk" the unexpected took a different, nasty turn.

Instead of a rational conversation, which ended with an agreement that we would try to treat each other better in the future, she took the opposite approach and began yelling at me the moment I opened the door. Speechless is a word that normally doesn't apply to me, but it did then. Flabbergasted is putting it mildly.

This is how she started her opening remarks. I'll kindly leave out the expletives. "How dare you make a scene in front of my friends! How dare you bring up Byron!" She continued with a few more, "How dare you's" but I didn't catch them because hearing that name come out of her mouth inspired a strange buzzing noise in my ears, which drowned out everything else. She did eventually calm down, sitting on the edge of the couch and holding her hands in her lap.

"Listen, Aster," she said. "Things have been bad for a really long time."

These little moments define our lives. Things happen that forever change your world. It's funny how you almost always know what you should do, how you should react, but pulling it off is something else. Wise men tell us that it's not what happens to you but how you react to what happens to you. I have known this for years and years and years, and have even managed to put it into practice a time or two. You bang your knee on an open drawer and you catch yourself mid-expletive and decide to laugh it off. These things are doable. This was not a situation I could easily laugh off. Maybe Socrates could pull it off. Epictetus could for sure, but not me.

It took her an hour to gather up the rest of her things. I sat and watched her, trying to get her voice out of my head, "Byron, Byron, Byron!" but failing miserably. I could feel something welling up inside me: something full of hatred and bad intentions. So I did what we mere mortals do: I succumbed to overwhelming temptation, flipped Socrates the bird, pushed Epictetus to the side and stormed out to find and beat the tar out of a perfectly innocent jackass.

MS. FISHER

Dearest Laverne:
  Stay away! Be glad we're not speaking face to face, dear. Nothing like a birthday to remind your immune system that it's due for a breakdown. When I got up this morning, I swear I'd been stomped on by a gang of angry four year olds. The soles of my feet itched and I could feel my ears without touching them, which is as weird as it sounds. I'm stuffed up as all heck, and my throat is the consistency of sandpaper. I keep trying to get someone to feel my head because if feels like I'm burning up, but they keep running from me. I must look really pretty.

You should come down here and feel my head. You've got such cold hands. I mean that in a good way. You should get them checked, though. Your circulation must be out of whack or something. It could be a symptom of something more serious, like an aneurism. Why else would you have corpse hands? Aren't we a pair: I've got drainage and you've got blockage…Oh well, I guess we'll die together. Do you want to hold my hand?

Sorry, it must be the medication. For some reason I was thinking that Nyquil is like cough drops. I took a dose before I got in the shower this morning, and then I took another one with my coffee, and then I took another one before I sat down to write you so I'm feeling woozy and kind of ornery. The cherry is really quite good. Anyway, you're not dying, I'm sure of it. And you don't have corpse hands. That was rude.

Anyway, it's nothing to worry about, dear, I'm just complaining. Everything has probably caught up with me. What with Art and the cookies and the flowers and Ernie and people stealing my broom and going into the doctor's office for tests every other day, of course I'm sick. So today is the one day I'm not scheduled to see the doctor and I have to go see the doctor because I've got pneumonia or something. And now I'm freezing. I actually shivered just then. If we were on the phone, you'd hear my teeth chattering.

Don't let me go to sleep! What an awful position to put you in, since you won't get this for a day or two. It's like when you're fishing and it's really cold out and your grandfather tells you that if you go to sleep you'll never wake up. Why would you say that to a seven-year-old? You know how long it used to take me to get to sleep in the winter time? And in the summer I would pile the blankets on and wake up in the morning with heat rash and dry mouth.

You really are a good friend, you know that? The best, really. In a sea of monsters, you are a really good fish. Not too many other people would put up with my ramblings…I think Ernie is in love with me. Why else would he remember my birthday? You know how I said I didn't want to remember my birthday? That's not true. I didn't want to remember because then I would know how many people forgot…My god, that's so sad.

But my little Ernie didn't forget. You should have seen the little hat he was wearing this morning. He ran away before I could tell him how cute he looked. He's amazing, even if he is short.

Your only friend,

B.A. Fisher

From the Archives
The Last Stop Bulletin

The Weather Front

The sun is once again shining, but it will take more than that to warm our hearts. It is odd, we know, to break the news of Mary's declining condition in The Weather Front, but we felt it would be odder still to bury it down in the You Ought to Know column.

Mary has fought the good fight, but it doesn't appear that this is a battle she can win. The doctor's won't put a time frame on it, but they assure us that she doesn't have long. We won't carry on in a way Mary would find sentimental and tiring, so we'll just let it be known that our hearts are collectively breaking and leave it at that.

Mary wouldn't like the idea of any of you sulking inside on such a beautiful day, so get out there and enjoy it. The following Weather Front is dedicated to Mary: It is going to be a gloriously beautiful, song-filled day with purple…turns out we're not very good at colorful prose.

Upcoming Events

As you may or may not know, Amato sometimes gets bored cooking our regular menu and occasionally tries experimenting with new and exotic dishes. We have heard through the grapevine that he is working on something that's never been tried on this continent, so you are hereby warned. We just hope it's legal. Sometimes these experiments are not a smashing success, so if you don't like it, please, please, please don't mention it to him, simply scrape your plate into the trash when he's not looking. Need we remind you that Amato doesn't do criticism? On a lighter note, Amato is now trusting Nathan to cook the eggs and hash browns by himself. Good for you, Nathan!

You Ought to Know

Now that the heat is on (wasn't that a song?) it's only fitting that the air conditioning go on the fritz yet again. We're starting to sound like a broken record. We don't want to second guess our super-hero maintenance man, but we've started taking a hard look at the budget to see if we can replace the whole unit. We know all about the horrible timing of it all, and so does Harry, so don't bring it up unless you want him to crank up the heat in your room. He's done it before. It will be fixed, Harry tells us, when it's fixed, and if anyone is planning on asking him about it, they should do it over the phone from Tahiti.

The Hot Seat

For God's Sake, Ms. Crocker! Think of the animals! They are fighting amongst themselves, and there have been casualties. Have you seen the corpses? Two of the bigger squirrels went at it and now one of their little legs is out there on the sidewalk attracting flies. If you want to see it you'll have to be quick because one of the horned owls has his eye on it. Do you see what you've done? You are putting all of their lives in danger. Some of the smaller hopefuls (rabbits, raccoons, frogs, etc.) are in danger of being trampled by the stampeding mule deer. Stop it!

The Suggestion Box

You have spoken and we have listened, but that doesn't necessarily mean Harry has listened or is even interested. A lot of you have been asking, some would say badgering, us about when the new stamina stairs will be done. WE DON'T KNOW. If you want an answer, put on your heavy body armor, strap on your helmet, check that your health insurance is up to date, and ask the man himself.

HOLY MOSES!

This is truly a dark day for our boy. What with the ear and Mary, he is nearly beside himself. He might not know how to type or sing Christmas carols, but he knows when something is wrong, and considering he's parked himself in front of Mary's suite, he knows a bit more than that. And as far as the Christmas carols go, we've still got six months to work on it.

CASSANDRA

Something tells me things aren't going to work out between me and
Eric. I don't mean to laugh, because he's nice and all that, but dinner
started with him telling me about how he always wanted an Orange
Roughy as a pet and ended with him trying to feed me some of his
steamed vegetables. I don't like being fed. You should have seen me,
when he came in for the force-feed I karate chopped his hand and one of
the green beans ricocheted off his crazy, velvet, Dracula collar and landed
in his water. He spent the next ten minutes trying to fish it out with his
fork. And then, without thinking, obviously, he said, "What will you do
if I get it out?" And I said, "Well, I'm certainly not going to touch it, if
that's what you're thinking," and took the glass from him and gave it
to one of the busboys. That was the highlight of the evening, and it was
completely lost on him.

I don't think Eric has much practice when it comes to dating. If I
was evil and horrible, I'd tell him that it might have something to do
with his cologne smelling like something he stole from his grandmother's
perfume box. I haven't been that embarrassed for someone since Vernon
woke me up in the middle of the night and told me that he was going to
quit his one and only decent paying job and write a mystery novel with
a detective named, you guessed it, Vernon, who would cleverly go by V,
and solve crimes using sunglasses that allowed him to see people's secrets.

So, needless to say, it was an early night. That's all right, though,
it gave me time to finish this book I started called, "Talent, What is
it Good for?" I haven't come up with a way to get out of the recital

without disappointing a lot of people, so I figure I better get some help. The good news is that according to the book, talent is way overrated. All you really need to do is practice. Good news, right, because obviously I'm not exactly overflowing with musical talent. But according to this guy you have to practice for 10,000 hours to get really, really good at something. But I don't have to be really, really good, I just don't want people throwing things. But half that is still a crazy long time, which, obviously, I don't have. How many hours do you think it'll take me to get just above stinky?

The other problem is that you can't just practice. You have to practice deliberately, meaning you have to identify your weaknesses and concentrate on those. My problem is that my weaknesses are so completely overwhelming that I don't even know where to start. You'd think that in the process of identifying my weaknesses I'd run across a couple of strengths, but no…I can't wait to see what sort of dreams I'll have with all this new pressure. The way I tend to deal with stress is by having really weird dreams. Last night I had a dream that Eric was looking down at me and his freckles began separating from his face and dancing around my head. And then his collar suddenly sprang to life and turned into a giant poinsettia. The most disturbing part isn't the disembodied freckles or the poinsettia, but the fact that he was looking down at me, which means he was over me, which means we could have been…There are a couple of things that I will never, ever do, not ever: watch The Exorcist by myself, and That with someone who reminds me of the time I had gum and peanut butter in my hair at the same time. I'm telling myself that I had fallen trying to stop his stupid Orange Roughy from jumping out of the tank and Eric was just helping me up.

So you ready for the punch line? I don't know what it is about men, but they can convince themselves of anything. Eric apparently told himself that we had a great date, because he asked me to a movie tonight. We were standing at my apartment door, and I was just about to apologize for our evening not working out when he said, "Hey, that was great. How about a movie tonight?" First I made sure he was serious, and then I told him as gently as I could that I didn't see things working out between us, that there was no real connection, and that he was a great guy, and all the other lies women tell men to try and get them to go away without provoking the B word. I guess Eric hasn't been on enough dates to know when someone is saying, "Enough is enough," because he then suggested that he come over for the dreaded practice session, and I was so confused that I agreed, so he's bringing his Sony over at seven tonight and I suddenly feel like crying.

Aster

Prison, my friend, is no place for a person of distinction. Riffraff and the like are perfectly at ease with the cement walls and the open latrines. They sleep easy while drunks babble about lost love and perverts and drug fiends are thrown down on the bench next to them. Not my cup of juice at all. If I'm ever in that position again, I'll take my chances with door number two, thank you very much.

I found Byron in the theater catching an early showing of a Charles Bronson movie, the name escapes me. Perhaps it was the nature of the action on the screen, or the tension-filled soundtrack, but I didn't hesitate. As soon as I spotted him, I attacked. I had the element of surprise already, but imagine his real surprise when I took his head in my hands and started gnashing at his ear like a dog with an old slipper. Unconventional, I know, to go with biting straight off, but I was inexperienced at combat and it seemed the natural thing to do. He yelped and bucked and cursed and thrashed, but I held fast, and when the ear lost its appeal, I pounded the top of his head with the palm of my hands until he became dizzy and went over sideways into the aisle. The pent up rage of a lifetime was released when I flipped him over and pounded on his chest with both fists. I yelled and laughed until I lost my equilibrium and fell sideways, pulling Byron on top of me. He seemed content to just lay there smothering me, so using the strength I had developed from my pushups, along with the massive amounts of adrenaline surging through me, I pressed him off me and flung him to the side.

One of his fingernails caught me just above the left eye, and a river of blood and goo not seen since Hannibal's march across Carthage oozed into my eye and down the side of my face, blinding me to the ensuing chaos. I am told that the paramedics rushed in and that Kelly launched herself off one of the chairs like a WWF wrestler and pinned me to the ground. The police came in after that, their clubs drawn and twitching, and whisked me off to the station.

You would never think me a jailbird, but there you have it. Byron didn't press charges, bless his soul, so there were no court appearances or orange jump suits. I was released early the next morning to Randy who lured me into a high-five and a knuckle-bump.

Looking back, I'm not proud, exactly, but later, after the burning and the soreness and the ringing in my ears went away, I felt light on my feet. Once you have survived the gladiatorial games you have a new perspective on things.

Despite being concerned about my general well-being after the fight, Ruby still hadn't changed her mind. We did talk some, though. And it was during this conversation that she tried to explain things.

"Well, Aster, I didn't think you had it in you, but you finally managed to surprise me. It's a shame, though. I was never with Byron, you dummy. We happened to be in the pool at the same time and I forgot my towel. That might be considered an affair in other countries, but not here. I knew what everyone was saying. But I would never be with Byron, you fool, and the fact that you didn't know that is a great example of what's wrong with us. The truth is, I'm not with anyone. I'm by myself for the first time in forever and I like it. I'm sorry to have to tell you that, but our life had become the same day, the same conversations, the same… everything, and when you're closer to the end than to the beginning, to continue on that way —I couldn't do it anymore. I think this is the best thing for both of us."

All I could manage to say was, "So I've lost my wife, and I've pummeled an innocent man."

"He had it coming a hundred different ways. Besides, now you're a hero."

Not quite. The beating I gave Byron actually only amounted to a dozen-or-so superficial scrapes and a couple of bruised ribs. I learned a few things about myself, though, not the least of which was that I was a dummy and a fool with no talent for hand to hand combat.

Ms. Fisher

Dearest Laverne:
    Sorry about my last letter. The last time I had that much Nyquil I went into a 7-eleven and threatened the manager with my shoe when he refused to refill the nacho cheese machine. At least I wasn't operating heavy machinery or driving a bus or something. I lose all judgment when I'm sick. My head gets all fuzzy and I go all cockeyed.

But that's old news. You should see my new dress. I bought it yesterday. Randy took us to Saks Fifth Avenue. I know, hotsy totsy, right? I haven't been there in years and years, and they're even more expensive than I remember, but you know what? I told myself, listen, you're not getting any younger, it's been eons since you treated yourself to a new outfit, and purple is your favorite color, so what the heck. You know it's the things you don't do that you end up regretting. I would have come back here and stewed about it and then probably hopped on an eight o'clock bus only to find that someone had snatched it in the meantime. See, now I can die happy and they can bury me in my pretty new dress.

I've already been complemented on it three times today. I bumped into Ernie coming out of the library, and before he could talk himself out of it, he told me I looked ravishing. I think that's what he was trying to say: all I heard was, "Rav—" and then his voice caught and he slammed the door on my foot. Little Ernie thinks I'm ravishing…imagine that. I know what you're thinking: again with the cold medicine. He's so timid. I'm going to bring out the inner man in him if it's the last thing I do. He has to be in there someplace. And then if I can get the inner man to give the outer man a few pointers, starting with his hair and those crazy glasses he wears, well, then we'll be on our way. A little coordination and a social skill or two wouldn't hurt, but I don't want to get greedy. Now that I think about it, though, it would help if he could eat in front of people and make eye contact every now and then. I'm not asking for Cary Grant, for crying out loud…Do you think he'd be willing to change his name? I'm not a big fan of Ernie. I don't know anyone who is, come to think of it. I wish I knew his last name. Maybe he has a strong last name like Barren or Harding. Or Walker, like Walker, Texas Ranger.

And if all that isn't enough to think about, my daughter is coming to visit tomorrow afternoon. You can imagine my excitement. That didn't come out right. I should try it with a more cheerful, optimistic tone. My daughter is coming to visit! I'm horrible, I know. I should be happy. When other people say, "My daughter is coming to visit," they have a twinkle in their eye.

She left a message with Beverly. Isn't it peculiar how she never calls me directly? I don't see how we're possibly going to mend our relationship if she always has to use a go-between. I have no idea what we're going to talk about, but I figure, at the very least I can ask her about the cookies and find out why her creepy husband was here the other day.

Your only true friend,

B. A. Fisher

From the Archives
The Last Stop Bulletin

The Weather Front

Glorious sunshine, blah, blah, blah, couple of white puffy clouds later in the afternoon, more sun, but not enough to burn, blah, blah, blah, beautiful sunset around eight, blah, blah, blah, pleasantly cool this evening, blah, blah, blah, perfect sleeping weather, blah, blah, blah... How quickly we change our tune. Isn't it rough living in Colorado?

Upcoming Events

Finding nothing worth mentioning, we have decided to relate a concern from our most concerned resident, Luther M., who brought it to our attention that the seatbelts in the transport van are attached to the seats themselves...We'll let that sink in for a moment...There's no need to spell it out, you can easily see why that might not be ideal. Not really an Event yet, but it certainly would be if you suddenly found yourself airborne on your very own ejector seat. Rest easy, Luther, we're looking into it.

You Ought to Know

Ah hem...We wish we had better news, but Ms. Verney is back in the hospital, this time for multiple puncture wounds to both ears, and a nasty gash above her left eye that will require several stitches to close up. How the bee got into Beauty Inc. and why Katelyn went after it so aggressively with the scissors, catching our beloved Ms. Verney in the crossfire, we don't know. Maybe she's allergic. Katelyn is despondent and we have been unable to remove the scissors from her clenched fist. If she doesn't snap out of it soon, we'll have no choice but to admit her for evaluation. Before word spreads, it was not a blood bath. There was blood and quite a bit of screaming, but nothing along the lines of *Friday the Thirteenth*. Katelyn is not a killer; she just really doesn't like bees.

THE HOT SEAT

Normally, this would be in The Suggestion Box, but due to the heinous nature of the suggestion, we have no choice but to put it here. We're sorry, Mr. Parker, we know you are a good person, but we feel that in desperation to be included in The Suggestion Box, you have gone too far. You have had some excellent ideas over the years, but the idea of lobbing off Holy's other ear in an attempt to trick him into thinking there is nothing wrong with the first one, feels, to us anyway, like something from the fourth century. We know your heart is in the right place, but really, did you think it through? It wouldn't work anyway. You're forgetting who you're dealing with.

THE SUGGESTION BOX

You have spoken and we have listened. Well, we don't know what she did, but after one week of driving, we received no fewer than thirty-five suggestions to keep Julie on permanently as a backup driver. None of you elaborated, but we gather that Jules, as you refer to her, is gobs of fun. We offer no guarantees, but with such overwhelming enthusiasm, we will take the suggestion seriously and will put in a good word for her. With Mary and Ms. Verney in the hospital, and Holy's weekly vet trips, there is no shortage of work, so, at least for the time being, you can keep her.

HOLY MOSES!

Mr. Moses is slowly returning to his old self. He is still self-conscience about the ear, so try not to stare, and if you touch it, he will plead with you to make it grow back. His hearing in that ear also seems somewhat diminished; if you stand on his right side without him knowing you are there and yell, he will look over his left shoulder. This should be temporary.

CASSANDRA

I've got two words for you: *Endless Love*. Are you kidding me? Lionel Ritchie and Diana Ross? You don't know it? How do you not know it? Everybody knows it. I don't even think I was born when it came out, and I even know the lyrics: "My Love…there's only you in my life…the only thing that's right…" See, I told you. This is a freaking catastrophe. We're playing some other songs, too. *Crocodile Rock* is one of them, which seems like it would be hard but at least there's other instruments and people will be drunk and dancing by then and not paying attention to me. But we're opening with *Endless Love* and I'm going to have to carry the whole song. You know how I punch the keys when I'm nervous. How's that going to sound?

I will say this, though: Mary Ann and Mr. Ukley are going to be singing it, and they've got amazing voices, so maybe if I play really quietly it'll sound okay. I don't even know how to play the song, and now I have to learn how to play it softly? God!

Sorry I freaked out on you. I have a really bad habit of imagining the worst. I just don't like looking and feeling silly, especially in front of people. I'm trying to work on it. I really like the idea of being a positive person…Maybe Eric can help me.

He came over last night, by the way. There was a moment when I wanted to turn off all the lights and act like I wasn't home, but then I looked out the peephole and he looked so excited, and he had wine, which is a huge plus, so I took a deep breath and let him in. He's still not the stuff boyfriends are made out of—at least not for me—but he's nice and he's funny once he relaxes. He wasn't all dressed up, either, and he didn't talk about fish, which was nice. Some people just look better in jeans and a t-shirt.

You know what he said? I played what I could of *Moonlight Sonata* for him and when I was done, he said totally deadpan, "Wow, you really are bad," and we both cracked up. And then he "played" and he couldn't even finger a chord. He's only been playing for like fifteen minutes, but he sucks sure as nothing and it made me feel better. When he was leaving, he gave me an awkward hug and whispered, "Friend's forever," in my ear and then he said, "What am I saying? I don't even like you." I think we'll get along just fine.

He's got a serious side, though. After we'd played around awhile, he started telling me about his family and how his sister had recently been attacked walking out to her car, and when she wouldn't give up her car keys, the guy beat her pretty badly. How's that for a change of subject? Your smile died right there in front of me. Sorry. Anyway, it would have been worse, he said, but a couple walking their dog saw what was going on and scared him away. She lives in Ohio. I just mention that, because I didn't want you to think it happened right down the street or something. And nothing against Ohio, it's just a fact. Anyway, it freaked me out a little bit, because he started giving me statistics about violent crime in our area. Our building isn't in the best part of town, and he said that I should take a self-defense course since I'm so pretty and would probably be a target. I've never thought of myself as a target before.

Anyway, long story short, there's a self-defense class down at the YMCA that I'm going to take this weekend. You never know when you're going to get mugged, right? And being how I'm so pretty and everything…

ASTER

"Byron is among the living! Our shirtless leader has returned from the infirmary! He's a pint or two low, but who needs blood when you draw strength from your hair! What a guy! Now who wants candy apples?" This I announced to the restaurant patrons upon Byron's return. I clapped and tried to whistle, but I've never been a good whistler. I'm not prone to heartless taunting, but seeing Byron, man among men, flexer of muscles, shameless lady killer, dressed in long sleeves and struggling with the salad tongs, was too much to be ignored. He looked by all appearances as though he would drop to the ground and soil himself if his shadow snuck up on him and said, "Boo!"

And his troubles weren't over. Later that day he had to return to the hospital because one of the scratches on his stomach had become infected. For this, I was blamed. It was my fingernail, after all, which had caused the wound, and they felt that Byron was having trouble recovering because of all the stress he was under. They even suggested he get a restraining order against me since I was the chief stressor in his life.

All of this brings back my college days, when I was a fully haired young man studying psychology at the University of Denver. If I could hop in a time machine, I would use Byron's case for my midterm paper. It is fascinating: Before a series of unfortunate events—its climax being his flopping around in the rosebushes, which I'll get to later—Byron was a pillar of strength, of confidence, of intensity and power. if he had been alive in Roman times, they would have made a statue in his honor. He was unstoppable. If you asked anyone what they thought of Byron, they would say—after the obligatory, "but he's a jackass,"—that he was an example of someone who saw no limitations, was undaunted by age, and welcomed adversity with open arms.

Now, this same fellow, this same collection of skin, muscle, hair and brains, the same Being whom we've just admitted was a shining example of the man's man, had been reduced to an awkward preteen, averting his eyes, stammering, tripping over his own feet. Why should this be? Confidence is everything. Once shaken, it is hard to coax out of the corner. And Byron's confidence hadn't just been shaken, it had been shattered and danced upon, as evidence by his tripping over the smallest cracks in the sidewalk while trying to recall the runner he once was, and his unwillingness to confront me when I laughed and pointed at him. There was nothing physically different about him. He was still the mighty Byron on the outside, but his brain had turned against him. He had no opponent, yet through his own self doubt, he was beaten. I did not defeat Byron; Byron defeated himself.

Now, if we turn it and see how this same experience affected me, we can learn something else about human nature. While I knew deep down that I had not hurt Byron, not really, and what damage I had done had more to do with the element of surprise than with any skills I may have had. Had I not been in a near frantic emotional state, had it not been dark, had he not been seated with his back to me, things no doubt would have played out differently. However, this was not common knowledge. Only Byron and I knew the real circumstances. So when news spread that I had beaten Byron to the tune of an ambulance ride, I was elevated to the level of superhero.

This too has a remarkable effect on confidence. I began walking differently. I treated people with indifference and scoffed at their limitations. I had aspirations of starting a senior boxing league, complete with tournaments and title fights. I saw myself taking on all comers, one after another, like Louis Gossett Jr. in *Diggstown*. I began hitting the weights more frequently and reading books on various martial arts. I began seeing myself as a weapon. This, of course, is complete, blithering nonsense. Now, in my defense, part of the reason I was acting out this way was to take my mind off Ruby, which it did, but in the process, I had replaced Byron as idiot-in-residence.

Ms. Fisher

Dearest Laverne:

I could use some ICYHOT this morning. Do I complain a lot? Sorry, dear, it seems like I start every letter with some sort of grievance, so today I'm going to break the mold and ask you, "How are you this morning, my oldest, dearest, sweetest friend?" You mentioned in your previous letter that you had an ingrown toenail that was acting up. How's that going? In my experience, anything "ingrown" can't be good. You'll pull through, though. You always do. I just hope it hasn't put a stop to your morning walks. I wish I could get up like you do, but I've always thought that sunrises were better imagined than seen. When are you going to send me a picture of you and that Service Dog, Barney the Labrador, you keep telling me about? He's going to have a tough time outdoing Holy Moses, but I mostly believe you when you say he's the most darling dog ever.

Anyway, what I shouldn't tell you but will anyway because I have to find someone to feel sorry for me, is that I fell asleep on the recliner and two things happened: one, my watch got hung up on the fabric behind my head and I apparently spent most of the night trying to yank it free, because it feels like my shoulder's been popped in and out of the socket a few times; and two, I think a bug crawled in my mouth and I ate it, because when I woke up this morning, the taste in my mouth was unimaginable. Thank god for Scope. It took four gurgles and four swallows to get rid of the taste. I'm trying not to think about it.

So, you're probably wondering how my daughter's visit went. She didn't show up. I know, not really surprising. But what was surprising was that Art the Fart showed up in her place. That's the last time I open the door without first checking the peephole. I swear I yipped and jumped back three feet. I know I've called him a shape-shifter and speculated that he was a vampire, but that doesn't give you an accurate picture of him. And that Christmas picture I sent you makes him look much more attractive than he actually is, even with the crazy eyes.

He is short. I know I've mentioned that before, but I can't stress it enough. I am five-six and a half, and I tower over him like an Amazon lady. And because of this, I have a birds-eye view of his shiny head. The hair that should be on his head has relocated to his knuckles, neck, chest, arms, and back, though I haven't had the pleasure of confirming the last one. Now, hold that image in your mind, and picture him in stocking feet and shamelessly intoxicated and crying and you'll have some idea of what I opened the door to. The smell, Laverne, the smell…was appalling. I don't know if it was from whatever was stained all over his shirt and pants, or because he obviously hadn't seen soap and hot water for several days or even weeks. With all the hair sprouting up all over the place, you'd think his beard would come in normal, but it came in uneven and patchy. Now do you see why I yipped?

What could I do? I let him in. I'm not that cold-hearted. He'd been crying, for heaven's sake. I had to at least find out what all that was about or it would drive me up the wall. I'm always interested in what makes men cry. That on top of the fact that he had obviously stopped bathing was too much intrigue to ignore.

So, you know me: I'm not one for chit-chat except with the chosen few, but as soon as I got him inside and sitting down I began pelting him with questions: Why are you snooping around? Why do you smell? Where's Jennifer? Why do you like to look up women's dresses? Why are you trying to kill me? What the heck was with the cookies? Why do you smell? Have you been drinking? What in God's name is all over your shirt? Do you know you smell?

All reasonable questions. He wouldn't answer me, though, and I couldn't stand the aroma, so I ordered him into the shower, gave him a couple towels I was saving for Goodwill, and told him to throw away the soap when he was done.

Your only true friend,
B. A. Fisher

From the Archives
The Last Stop Bulletin

SPECIAL ANNOUNCEMENT

For those of you that don't already know, Mary Stuart passed away early this morning surrounded by friends and family. It was swift and painless. Her last words were to one of her grandkids who inquired why she had to go away: "I'm ninety-three years old, little dear. I have taken up space long enough," which was followed by the laugh we all came to love. Today's Bulletin is dedicated to her memory.

The Weather Front

Sunshine…That's the best we can do. We aren't feeling overly creative today, so we're afraid that's going to have to suffice…We could live in North Dakota where the word of the day would be Snowdrift, so don't complain.

Upcoming

We have removed "Events" from the heading for today's column, because "Event" implies something to look forward to. Mary will be laid to rest in Fairmount Cemetery next to her mother and grandmother. There will be a viewing and a celebration of her life Wednesday evening, but we haven't received all the details. Obviously, when we know, you will know.

YOU OUGHT TO KNOW

Sorry to all those who lobbied so hard for *Some Like it Hot*, but this week's movie has been changed to *Casablanca*, Mary's favorite. "Of all the gin joints in all the towns in all the world, she walks into mine," in case you needed reminding. *Some Like it Hot* will be back on the big screen next week.

THE HOT SEAT

We're really not in the mood this morning. Anything we could come up with would seem trivial and silly considering the circumstances, so rest easy…but not for too long. We'll be back tomorrow with the brass knuckles on.

THE SUGGESTION BOX

Harry has suggested we hang photographs commemorating The Last Stop and the Riley family in various parts of the building. This will give visitors, not to mention residents, an appreciation of what The Last Stop and the Riley family have stood for all these years. Harry may be gruff and man of few words, but he never ceases to astonish us. We will begin the process immediately. Oh, yes: You have spoken and we have listened.

HOLY MOSES!

Holy Moses is home and recovering from his adventures. He was escorted home by Harry, who no doubt gave him a good tongue lashing. Harry found him soaking wet, trying to figure out how to scale Violet's new privacy fence. Apparently he took a shortcut through the river. The bandage that should have been on his ear had slid down and was covering one eye. To think that he dove into the same river that almost drowned him as a puppy, swam (we don't know how considering his girth) to the other side, scampered up the bank, picked his way through the trees and brush, crossed four lanes of traffic, and found Violet's house, which, we

might add, looks exactly like every other house in that subdivision, is…
well, not entirely surprising.

CASSANDRA

Sometimes I just find a tree and sit with him. It's like therapy, only you don't have to worry about the therapist suddenly suggesting you do jumping jacks for some weird reason. All he does is listen. And all he asks is that you toss him a cheese cracker every now and then. See, he's listening to us right now…really listening. The world could learn a thing or two from Holy Moses.

So, I've been out here asking Holy for advice. He's a little short on words, so I'll ask you, too. Vernon sent me something in the mail today that goes against everything I know about him. I thought for sure he'd do his time planning a bank heist or something equally stupid…but according to this, he's actually been working hard.

I know it's just a GED, but up until now, I wasn't even sure he could read…and look at this, "The Bells, a Study in Meter, by Vernon Baker." By Vernon Baker? Meter? I didn't even know what that meant until I read his paper, so now I have officially learned something from Vernon and I want to barf. Come on, he's reading poetry? Vernon with a V studies things—anything?

I couldn't believe it so I called his mother and she confirmed everything and told me that she couldn't wait for me to see his new look, as if it's a foregone conclusion that I'll agree to see him. And get this: he's writing some of his own poetry, stuff that came out of his own head. The only poetry I can picture Vernon writing would go something like this: "I like Hash, I like Mash-ed…Potatoes with my Hash…Browns." She said I'll be so proud of him. I love that woman, but I think she's sick.

So here's my question: Can people change? I mean really change. Or do they always go back to the way they were. I have to give him credit: it's not like he read Green Eggs and Ham over the weekend and is now trying to convince me that he's a scholar. He spent a lot of time and worked really hard on this…And this paper? It's not great, but he's got most of his commas in the right place and he seems to know what he's talking about.

I know: I found classical music and the piano, so I guess it's conceivable that he found poetry, but this is Vernon with a V we're talking about; the Vernon that steals lawnmowers from old guys and answered my question, "Where would you go if you could go anywhere in the world?" with "Utah, to see the Amish people up close."

Okay, so I saved the best for last. Look at this little note he attached to the diploma: "I did this for myself, but I couldn't have done it without you. You are my because." If you ignore the last part, it's a really nice thing to say. It's got me all screwed up. If he wrote, "All for you, baby," and spelled baby with three b's, then it would make sense, but this…I think he's sincere. And if I ignore him he'll probably keep doing these sorts of things. There's no way he could write this paper and go back to being the Vernon that I know. I think Vernon with a V is dead.

Why is he doing this to me? I'm supposed to run into him five years from now so he can see what he's missing. But, no, my Vernon has to go and better himself…the jerk.

ASTER

This, my friend, is the Crumb-catcher 5000! Go ahead and tell me it stinks and watch how I laugh at you. This is what the world has been waiting for.

Isn't it a wonderful morning? I was up early cooking waffles and eggs and toast. Ruby used to do most of the cooking. When I offered to help her she would say, "No, no, dear. I'm quite hungry." But something about waffles inspires me to break out the rusty toaster and the butter spray. And after looking at the toaster for a long while and silently cursing the crumbs that seemed to rain down all over the counter from parts unknown, it reminded me of an idea I had had over thirty years ago for a crumb-catcher.

Just like Martin Luther King Jr., I had a dream. Mine was less ambitious but just as sincere. But while MLK didn't allow anyone to stand in the way of his vision, I let my cousin convince me that my idea was foolish. It's pure insanity how we let the opinions of others stop us from doing what we want to do. You must understand that I thought my crumb-catcher was a breakthrough on par with the q-tip or the paper clip. Every household would have one. I drew up plans and was trying to come up with a catchy jingle for marketing when I made the mistake of telling said cousin about it, who proceeded to roll his eyes and tell me I'd be better off designing a crumb-less bread.

The lesson of the day: Hold your dreams tight, my friend. Share them with no one. And when the naysayers and the scoffers of the world aren't paying attention, spring it on them fully formed and laugh and dance while they grasp desperately for a hand-hold with which to drag you down. Impossible, someone once said, is an opinion, and I for one would like to shake his or her hand.

Now, I don't want you to think ill of this particular cousin. He is blood, after all, and usually a very supportive fellow, if a little dry. He was simply trying for a little humor, which is not his strong suit. There is a time and place for sarcasm, but only for those who know how to use it correctly. And the poor guy had no idea what he had done.

Now, like I said, I had already been thinking about the crumb-catcher, so imagine my surprise when said cousin called me straight out of the bright blue sky and very casually during the course of our conversation said, "Hey, why didn't you ever go through with that toaster thing? You probably could have made a killing." Oh, how I laughed and began thinking of clever ways of disposing of his corpse.

The world works in mysterious ways, and I for one am not going to fight it. If the cosmos wants a Crumb-catcher 5000, than a Crumb-catcher 5000 it shall have.

It's a shame to learn lessons late in life. Had it not been for that simple attempt at humor from someone who should have known better, my life might have taken a different path. I could have traveled the world, speaking before world leaders, showing them how my crumb-catcher, in its own small way, could help them with their Foreign Policy. I could have had that quaint little house in upstate New York with the hammock on the porch. I could have afforded a funny, little, wise maid named Lilly or Rita who would become world-renowned for her lemonade. But it is never too late!

So again, here it is. I am open to suggestions, but outright criticism will be met with an icy stare. Notice the ribbed edges and detachable crumb ramp. This is just the beginning. They will come in a variety of colors for all your toasting needs and will be completely universal. No toaster yet designed will be free from the Crumb-catcher attachment. Now, if I can just come up with a jingle…

Ms. Fisher

Dearest Laverne:

Sorry to end so abruptly, but you know who walked in and I didn't want him to see what I was writing. People in general don't like to read about how they're short and hairy. Yes, I'll end the speculation: Art has been staying with me the last couple of days. It turns out that the little runt was hanging around here trying to get up the courage to come and talk to me. Of courage he has almost none, so he's been sleeping down by the river and sneaking leftovers out of the trashcans. Eating trash and sleeping with the wildlife is preferable to knocking on my door. Maybe I haven't lost my edge.

So, long, long, long, story short. Art and Jen are having problems. Actually, he's the one with the problem because she threw him out. And as much as I hate to admit it, after hearing his side of the story, it's hard not to take his side.

Okay, you know how much I hate being wrong, so I'm just going get this over-with and throw it out there and you can laugh and make jokes if you must: Art is tolerable. Once he's cleaned up and his clothes are washed and he's sober, he's not nearly as offensive as I remember him. I still couldn't take his beard, so I borrowed a razor from Ernie, who looked on the verge of fainting when he opened the door, but he got his color back when I said I was just there for a razor. Apparently this isn't as odd a request as I thought it was because he slammed the door and returned a moment later and opened the door just enough to throw a disposable Bic out into the hall. I wonder if he thinks women like to have the door slammed in their faces. If I could catch him, I would ask him, but he's quick like a gazelle and I don't run for anybody...

So why do you think she threw him out? Infidelity? Drugs? Abuse? No, no. He made the mistake of suggesting that she get a job. I had no idea, but the only way they've been surviving is because Art's been able to pick up double shifts at the tire plant, but now the company is cutting back on overtime. Apparently Jen threw a fit and told him that the house would go to pieces if she wasn't home to take care of it. I hate going on this way about my own daughter, but they don't have a house, they have a tiny, one-bedroom apartment, with a couch, two sitting chairs, and, unless they've upgraded, about four plates and two glasses. The only thing they have in abundance is silverware, because I got it for them as a "house" warming gift. I hate taking Art's side on this, or anything, but what exactly is going to go to pieces?

His next mistake was suggesting that they cut back on some of their other expenses. But the only extraneous expenses they have are Jen's. I don't know where she got this. She buys clothes and gets manicures and gets her hair done, and then spends all day in sweat pants. Art's third and final mistake was pointing this out and before he knew what hit him, he and all of his belongings were down in the lobby.

So there you have it. He has nowhere to stay and no money, so what am I supposed to do? He doesn't even have his Driver's License because he left his wallet back at the apartment and when he went back to get it she threatened to call the police. On top of all this, he has managed to lose his job; something about personal hygiene and substance abuse.

So I'm going to call her and if she doesn't answer the phone, I'm going to have Randy drive me over there, and if she doesn't answer the door, I'm going to have Randy kick it down. This has been coming a long time. I vowed to stay out of her business, but enough is enough, forever.

So, between Jen and Art and Ernie, I'm two steps away from the Looney Bin. I can't even do my normal workout routine because I'm so distracted. Kelly noticed and yelled, "Come on, Fisher! Quit going through the motions!" When that did no good, she unplugged my treadmill mid step and drug me over to one of the stability balls and made me balance on it Indian-style with my hands clasped underneath my legs so if I fell I wouldn't have time to unravel and catch myself. This, she told me, required me to clear my head and focus on nothing but balancing on the ball. "If you fall, I won't catch you," she said and stood there for a full five minutes watching me sweat. When I finally did a sideways somersault off the damn thing, she said, "I told you. Now, don't you feel better?" Surprisingly, I did.

Your only true friend,
B. A. Fisher

From the Archives
The Last Stop Bulletin

SPECIAL ANNOUNCEMENT

The Riley family would like to thank everyone who turned out to pay their respects. The Service was beautiful and a fitting tribute to Mary's life. They thank you for all the flowers and gifts, which took a sixteen foot U-haul to transport back home.

The Weather Front

Last night reminded us of that Garth Brooks song some of you are so crazy about: "The Thunder Rolls." Anyway, you don't need Garth Brooks to tell you it was thundering last night. If you don't know what we're talking about, you should get with your Care Provider and take a long hard look at your medication. And while we're at it, you don't need a meteorologist to tell you that it's dark and menacing-looking or that it's been drizzling since early this morning. However, we are here to tell you that the skies will clear, making way for a pleasantly sunny afternoon. We are also here to tell you that we have absolutely no basis for the above forecast; we're just being optimistic.

Upcoming Events

Independence Day! Fourth of July! Hotdogs, Roasted Peppers! Apple

Sauce! Fireworks! Ah, yes, fireworks. We know it's still a week out, but it's never too soon for everyone's favorite Handy Man's annual Fourth of July Plea. Because this might fall into the hands of a child, we have eliminated the expletives and have chosen to put his thoughts in our own carefully chosen words. So, in a nutshell, please, please, please, please remember that fireworks are for designated areas only. Anyone caught lighting so much as a sparkler anywhere near the grassy areas will be covered with peanut butter and tied to a tree to endure Holy Moses and whatever else lusts after peanut butter.

We joke because we love; Harry does not joke, nor does he love much, so unless you want to see how angry an angry Handy Man can get and want to be lectured on fiery graves and smoldering memories, keep your eyes on the little tots running around. We think Harry would make an exception for those under ten, but we can't be certain. You are hereby warned: Harry will be patrolling the grounds in his new trademark firefighting backpack, complete with two fire extinguishers and burn balm. The balm is for him, not you, so be careful.

You Ought to Know

Sheeeee's here! And a lot sooner than we expected so for all of you little chatterboxes developing conspiracy theories about who's going to replace Mary Stuart, you can throw away the power point presentation, because her name is Helen Watson and she will be here later today to tour the facility. We don't know much about her yet, but we're reasonably sure she's not a Satanist like some of you have suggested.

Rest assured that she's not going to be Mary Stuart's clone. This late in life, Change often becomes a four letter word, so, on the count of three, repeat after us...THERE ARE GOING TO BE CHANGES AND IT'S GOING TO BE OK.

You Ought to Know (cont.)

This just in: Helen, according to this paper that was so rudely thrown at us by someone who shall remain nameless, comes to us from the Windy City where she spent the last seventeen years working as Patient Care Manager for Brindle Acres, an upscale retirement community just outside Chicago. Before anyone starts in on us, we're aware that Brindle is a coat color often found in dogs, and, no, we haven't a clue what that has to do with old people. Oh, yes, there's a footnote: she doesn't drink calves blood, nor does she sacrifice small children.

THE HOT SEAT

This is for all the people who won't heed our warning and will think they can light a sparkler in some remote corner and get away with it. Every year there is one or two of you. We figure this way we can just copy and paste and save some time, so here we go: For god's sake, how many warnings, postings, testimonials, verbal ultimatums, tell-tale glances, fire drills, lawn signs, and newsletters do you need? When you violate the very simple Fireworks policy, who do you think Harry comes to first? Yes, your fearless leaders take the brunt of it because for some reason he thinks we are responsible for your actions, and because we love you all so much, we protect your identity if at all possible. This will not continue. So those of you who "slipped up," be advised that when Harry comes knocking, we will further aggravate him by leading him to your door, all the while poking him with a stick. And just for the record: blaming your helpless grandchildren elevates you to a whole new class of criminal.

HOLY MOSES!

As you know, we have the only dog on planet earth that runs towards fireworks. He looks forward all year to launching himself after bottle rockets and stomping on spinners, so we need to come up with something equally spectacular to distract him, while still keeping him involved. We all know how he likes to show off, so we fear that having Violet in the audience will only make things worse. Excluding him from the festivities is not an option. We don't want a hurt, plotting, vindictive Holy Moses on our hands. We are open to any and all suggestions.

THE SUGGESTION BOX

Yes, we're aware that today's update is out of order, but it works better this way, as you'll see in a minute. Okay, ready? You have spoken and we have listened. Our very own Ms. Haladay has anticipated today's Bulletin and has suggested that we simply explain to Holy Moses why it would be better if he didn't play with fireworks. Even with his ever-expanding vocabulary, we are skeptical, but we have learned that when it comes to Holy Moses, anything is possible, so let us know what you think. Perhaps if we worded it without using any negatives we'd have a shot. Once he hears, No, Can't, Shouldn't, Never, etc, he has trouble moving beyond it.

CASSANDRA

Make one move and I'll take your eye out! How was that? One of the things our self- defense instructor said we should do is to yell and make as much noise as possible, so I'm improvising. I was going for violent and gruesome, but I'm not very good at it.

The class was awesome. I figured they'd have some guy in camouflage and sunglasses showing us how to kick someone in the groin and that would be about it, but we didn't even do that. The instructor was this Italian guy named Marcus and he was big, but not really scary-looking, even though you know he could kill you. He didn't speak like a tough guy, either. He wore jeans and had tattoos, but he spoke like a college professor.

Most of the afternoon was spent talking about overcoming fear and obstacles and changing the way we think. He asked this one lady in the class if she could kill her attacker if necessary, and, like all of us, it made her really uncomfortable, but then he asked her what she would do if that same person was attacking her children and she said she'd rip his f-ing face off. That's how you had to think, he said. It worked for me, too: I pictured someone hurting my mom and before I knew it I was envisioning myself using all kinds of things as weapons, including a mallet, which was weird but effective.

And then he changed gears and did this whole thing about expectations. He said that you're motivated by your expectations. If you visualize a positive outcome, it will motivate you to act; if you're expecting a negative outcome, you'll keep putting it off. So he told us to think about something in the future that we were nervous about—creepy, right?—and instead of visualizing what's making us nervous, he said to look for what we're going to get out of it and focus on that. One example he used was running. He said he hated running more than anything in the world but he knew that it would make him more effective at his job as a police officer, so he ran. He looked past the immediate discomfort and focused on the bigger picture. That's why he says most people fail to get into shape and eat better: They fixate on how much they don't like exercising and how tired they're going to be and all the food they're going to have to deny themselves of instead of focusing on how great they're going to look and how wonderful they're going to feel.

I'm going back again this weekend because there was so much to take in and I don't even remember half of it. I tried to scribble a lot of it down, but I wasn't prepared to take notes, so I spent a lot of time digging through my purse looking for something to write with instead of listening.

The whole last part was about identifying if a fear is real or if it's something we've created in our minds. Too many people, he said, walk around all worked up about events and situations and conversations that haven't happened yet. I've heard "don't assume" and "don't worry about things you can't control," but it never really sunk in until now. Like, he said, if you're going into a meeting with your boss and you're anxious about it, you should only focus on what it is you want to say, not what you think his reaction is going to be. Control what you can control, he said over and over again, and throw the rest away. "Identify the concern, prepare for it, and then overcome it."

So you know what? I'm going to play Endless Love, and it's going to be loud and it's going to be great and if anyone says anything I'm going to kick their ass.

ASTER

I had a tense moment this morning when I had Mr. Nelson down the hall check on the internet to make sure no one had stolen my idea for the crumb-catcher and came across something called the crumb-strip. But it turned out to be this silly rubber contraption that you line your countertops with that supposedly draws the crumbs towards it. And after the liner is sufficiently crumby you peel it off and throw it away like flypaper. So the question is how crumby is crumby enough before you can justify pitching it? Too soon and it become too costly, and too late and no one will want to visit you.

Since you insist on talking about insects, I purchased a new lamp that has an open top so the bulb is exposed and I found that moths are drawn to it. It's really a horrifying prospect for the moths because first they pop, then they catch fire, then they smolder. I'm hoping one of them is able to stop himself before he hits the bulbs so he can stand guard and warn the others to stay away. The first time it happened, it was an entertaining curiosity, but after the tenth or twelfth one smolders, it begins smelling up the room.

And still speaking of insects, doesn't the rose garden look good? It wasn't always so. It took a while for them to come back after Byron landed in them and thrashed around. I remember mentioning something about the rosebushes previously, so I will end the suspense and finish the story. I told you how I had started making a game out of harassing Byron. As with any game that is taken too far, there comes a point when you must grudgingly admit that enough is enough.

This moment for me came about a week after the restaurant scene. I had spent the week sneaking up behind him and yelling his name and watching him shoot towards the ceiling. This grew tiresome, so I decided to ratchet it up a notch. I had taken note that Byron was trying desperately to regain his old self by throwing himself into his old routines. Every morning I watched him run and attempt various jumps and calisthenics with varying degrees of success, and on this particular morning he must have been feeling spunky because he eyed the rosebushes and took off towards them with long, confident strides, with a mind of hurdling them like he had done in the past. And just before takeoff, I decided to make my presence known by springing out from behind a tree on the other side of the bushes and waving my arms wildly.

This threw him off stride and before he could recover and change his course, he was upon the bushes where he made a feeble attempt at jumping over the lowest of the thorny branches, but got hung up and went down. I dare say he did quite a bit of writhing and yelling and, unfortunately, bleeding.

It was then that I said to myself, "enough is enough." Once a man has rolled around in the rosebushes, he has hit rock bottom and is ready to begin rebuilding. So I decided to experiment. After holding some of the nastier branches out of his way so he could pick his way out of the bushes without further injury, and carefully removing one of the nastier thorns from his eyelid, I wished him well with the half dozen- or- so thorns still stuck in various parts of his body and returned to my room, where I began devising a plan that would, through a couple of carefully choreographed incidents, help return Byron to the arrogant asshole he once was.

Ms. Fisher

Dearest Laverne:

My life is turning into a bad episode of All My Children. Just when I thought things couldn't get any more chaotic, the doctor's office calls and tells me to come down so they can go over my test results with me. It sounds innocent enough, but it was a new receptionist and I didn't like her voice. It was happy and reassuring on the surface but just underneath I could tell that she just assume I get hit by a bus.

As you know, I like to be the antagonist, so I got a little testy with her and said that this week was bad for me so why didn't she just go ahead and tell me the results over the phone. She sighed just like I knew she would, but then she said something I wasn't expecting. "Ms. Fisher, this really can't wait. You really need to come down this afternoon… everything's going to be fine." I don't know if it was the 'can't wait' or the dreaded "everything's going to be fine," but my stomach did a little dance. Answer me this: Has anyone anywhere ever said, "Everything's going to be fine," when everything is fine? So I told her that if everything was going to be fine, why couldn't the doctor give me the results over the phone, and she sighed really long, which irritated me to no end. I'm dying, and she's the one that's annoyed.

I don't know when things changed, but nobody seems to care anymore. Pretty soon the whole thing will be automated like it is when you call the phone company. "To find out if you have cancer, press one. If you've had a heart attack, press two. If you're bleeding out, scream, 'help me!' or stay on the line."

So, of course I'm thinking cancer, so I asked her where it was and how long I had live, because I like to get bad news over with. I might as well have asked her if she'd seen my house keys because she told me she'd see me that afternoon and hung up

Poor Randy had to put up with me all the way to the doctor's office. You know how I talk a lot when I'm anxious? I was also talking really loud, which was new. Randy took it all in stride. He could be a male nurse if he wanted to. All my talk of death didn't faze him. He looked at me in the rearview mirror and said, "If its cancer—which you don't know if it is—they'll get it out and you'll be fine. And if they can't they'll give you that stuff that makes you throw up and you'll lose your hair, and you'll be fine…" I told him that I wished everyone would stop telling me that I was going to be fine. "Okay," he said. "What's the worst that can happen? You could die. But what's so bad about that? You've had a good run." Smart ass. Getting it right out in the open like that made me feel better, though, and he did have a point.

So we get there and I'm expecting my regular physician but in walks "Dr." Jones, the little kid with the stethoscope that I stabbed with the fork. He was more nervous than I was: stammering all over the place and shifting his weight back and forth. I told you I don't like anticipation. If I'm dying, I just assume know it right off so I snatched the chart from him and took it with me into the bathroom and locked the door.

After I saw what was on it, I walked out and threw it at him. If I had a fork, I would have stuck it in his forehead. On my way out, I told the receptionist that she should be ashamed of herself. If there is one thing you should never ever do, Laverne, it's let someone think they have cancer. Not even for a moment. They can say all they want about not disclosing information over the phone and policies and all that crap, I don't care. At some point you have to do what's right, and damn the procedures.

So I'll end the suspense, dear. I don't have cancer, and I'm not dying. What I have is a bladder stone the size of a ping pong ball, which they think can be dissolved with medication but that may require surgery. Why it took them this long to find it when I've had umpteen ultrasounds over the last couple of months, I'll never know. So I figure I'll go back in for the medication when I calm down. If I go back now, I'm liable to smack somebody.

Your only true friend,
B. A. Fisher

From the Archives
The Last Stop Bulletin

The Weather Front

Someone left us an angry note suggesting that we spend too much time picking on North Dakota, and after giving it some thought, we grudgingly must agree. Certainly—though we can't prove it and know of no one who can—there is more in North Dakota than just snow. We hear there are even flowers this time of year, but they are skittish and dive for cover any time the wind blows.

The truth is we have no idea why we choose to pick on North Dakota while leaving other obvious targets unscathed. For instance, as far as we know, we have never mentioned Minnesota in our Weather Front... perhaps North Dakota is easier to spell, though looking at it now, we doubt it. So in the interest of fairness, here are some thoughts on other states notorious for long, harsh winters.

Montana, for instance, ND's smug neighbors to the west, boast about the beauty and the open spaces, but neglect to mention that they hold the record for the lowest temperature ever recorded in the lower 48 states.

And then we have New England. The skiing in Vermont; the Fall colors in Connecticut; Stephen King's house in Bangor...but no one ever talks about the four-foot, black snowdrifts mucking up the parking lots. They don't take pictures of those. Why should North Dakota be excluded from the destination calendar market that the New Englander's so thoroughly monopolize?

Yes, The Peace Garden State has been gypped. Louis L'Amour is from North Dakota for crying out loud. What were we thinking?

Oh, yeah, the high today will be 87.

UPCOMING EVENTS

Now that we've all gotten to meet Helen, we fear there will be all kinds of Upcoming Events, none good (See The Suggestion Box), but we don't want to speculate on what they might be. We'll keep you posted.

YOU OUGHT TO KNOW

So, they put Katelyn and Ms. Verney in the same hospital room… We'll give you a minute or two to ponder the consequences of such an action…Further details should be unnecessary, but we will divulge them anyway, since we need something to write about.

As you can imagine, they associate each other with pain and extreme terror, so it isn't surprising that they have both taken a giant leap backwards in their recovery. Katelyn had actually mouthed a few words to the doctors, but after seeing Ms. Verney with her head bandaged up, went into a bout of uncontrollable shaking and yipping unlike anything the staff had ever seen. Ms. Verney mistook this as a precursor to another attack and did her best to throw herself out the window. They are separated now, but both are having trouble sleeping. They keep waking up screaming for entirely different reasons.

THE HOT SEAT

We have changed the Hot Seat to the Hot Booth this morning in order for our multiple offenders to be sufficiently humiliated. The Literary Bandits have struck again. Everyone remain calm. Because of Ms. Crocker's animal exploits, they have operated in relative anonymity. But now they have gone too far. Someone (Michael, Todd, Linda,) did a little reorganizing of our library over night. For some reason, all the "popular" books have been snatched from their rightful alphabetical place and have been moved to the lower shelves over by the bathroom, which are usually reserved for ten-year-old issues of National Geographic. So if you have any books considered "not serious" that you wish to donate to the library, we suggest you hold off and keep them locked in a trunk for the time being, lest the thugs wrestle them away from you and throw them in the fireplace.

So hear us now, you little sneaks: We will never break up our fiction into literary clicks, not ever, so if you can't stand the idea of King and Koontz sharing a shelf with Kafka and Kennedy, we suggest you get your books elsewhere. You have exactly twelve hours to return things to the way they were or we will start adding Joyce and Proust to the stack of coloring books. We can get nasty if we need to.

THE SUGGESTION BOX

You have spoken and we have listened. In fact, so many of you have spoken on this topic that we have been dreading writing this column all morning. Yes, we know, we were there. Helen's visit last night was uptight and eerie, but we cannot vote her out. She is here to stay, so we should go against popular belief and give her a second chance to make a first impression. Maybe it was the lighting that made her look so severe. Perhaps she can't help that she's always squinting and her mouth is in a constant frown. Who are we to judge? And, yes, her tone isn't conversational and she doesn't seem approachable. But remember: thou who looks like a serial killer is not necessarily a serial killer.

HOLY MOSES!

Yikes. The rumors are flying. Don't panic. Helen said she was a cat person but she didn't say she had one. She also didn't say that she wasn't a dog person, but unless we totally misread her body language, she didn't have to. It seemed to us that she was looking at Holy Moses with a certain something in her eye. And it seemed to us that Holy was looking at her with a certain something in his eye, too, which stood our hair on end. We repeat: Yikes.

CASSANDRA

I think I scared Eric. You know how enthusiastic—some would say crazy—I was after my self-defense course? I was way worse with him because he was in my apartment and I stood in front of the door so he couldn't leave. He had no idea what he was getting himself into. I was totally in his face and talking really fast and throwing my hands around so much that he was actually flinching. I'm usually not *that* crazy, but I had been thinking about what I had learned all day and writing it down and coming up with scenarios so I could work through them, so by the time he came over I was all worked up and just started screaming at him. He also forgot the wine, which would have slowed me down some, so it's really his fault.

So I've been trying to take everything I've learned and apply it to the piano and it's really hard because I'm not used to it. But I'm trying. Every time I try a new chord or try to get my hands to stop doing the same thing, and I'm screaming, "You suck!" at myself, I stop, and remind myself that everyone sucks when they first start and if I keep with it and keep with it I'll be good. And I have to thank Eric because he came up with the world's most obvious idea that somehow escaped me. He was sitting there eating peanuts in a really annoying way, and just out of the blue he says, "Why don't you get Mr. Jenson to help you?"

Seriously, I make things so freaking hard sometimes. I never ask for help, I swear. Of course I should ask Mr. Jenson for help. He's only been playing piano for three hundred years. And, news flash, he probably already knows how to play the songs we're doing. It seems like I violate every one of Marcus's rules. One of the first things he said was, "If you keep telling yourself how hard something is and why you can't do it, why are you surprised when it's hard and you can't do it?" I think I'm going to get wallpaper that says that and do my whole apartment with it. The other one I like is, "If you don't have a plan, you plan to fail." Maybe I'll get that stamped on all my dishes.

Eric had another one of his infuriating ideas later—he was really on a roll—when I was telling him how I'd probably end up playing the song great, but then fall off the wobbly piano bench.

"So get another piano bench, or get someone to fix it. Jeez."

I told him to shut up and go home. If he wouldn't have added, "Jeez" at the end, I probably would have let him stay: crazy people don't like that fact pointed out to them. And he was right, of course. I was so busy telling myself, "Whatever you do, don't fall off the bench, don't fall off the bench," that I missed the obvious solution. Marcus said something about that, too, if I can find it…"Fixating is debilitating and causes you to lose focus of the big picture." I swear I have to read all of these eighteen times a day.

So Eric's been helping me in the meantime. He printed out the music for all the songs and we're learning the chords together. Not the actual melodies yet, but at least I'll know the changes before I see Mr. Jenson after work tonight. I think Mr. Jenson was feeling left out, so at least now he can still be part of things. I'm trying to come up with something else for him to do. Oh, I almost forgot. Look at this…Do you know who this is? I'll give you seven guesses, and if you haven't got it by then, you don't deserve to know. The one thing I left out about Vernon because I didn't want you to think I was shallow and superficial, was that he's really, really cute. Why do you think I put up with him for so long?

I know, Denzel, right? And you can't even see his muscles, which I'm sure are even bigger now, since most guys get muscles in prison. I've never seen him in glasses before, but he looks very…something. At least he doesn't have that glassy stare anymore. I swear it was like you could see the hamster wheel rolling around in there. That was probably from the drugs, though.

Now look at this. That paper I showed you about poetry, it's being published in a poetry review and they say they'd like to see more of his work. I don't know what's more shocking: Vernon having "work" or that he's being published. Anyway, this is the photo he's thinking about sending for the author photo. He wants to know what I think. He also wants me to help him on the author bio, since he can't exactly say, "Vernon with a V is a convicted felon that recently gave up drugs and has since discovered the wonders of the written word…" I figure we'll keep it short and to the point: Vernon Baker lives and works in blah, blah.

ASTER

I have a bit of inside information if you promise to keep it under wraps. Kelly is planning some major changes to the Fitness Center and some of the programs. Good news. All those heinous fake bicycles and ridiculous revolving sidewalks that are lined up are going away for good, and I say, "Good day, sir!" Kelly noticed, like I had some years ago, that there are roughly eight hundred miles of walking and bike trails right down the hill from here, and realized how silly it is that we all line up on these contraptions in the confines of a building, breathing recycled air, and staring down at the wildlife and natural obstacles waiting for us.

But you mustn't breathe a word of this to anyone. All of this I overheard and I suspect that Kelly wouldn't react kindly to eves dropping, nor would the Green Giant that tags along with her sometimes. It has yet to be approved, but she's trying to add top of the line mountain bikes and walking sticks to her arsenal of weights and stability balls. And along with teaching all of us how to safely fall off our bikes, she is going to start a boot camp for those of us that can't stick to a routine on our own and respond well to verbal abuse. Don't let it intimidate you. I have weathered Kelly's worst and I'm here to tell you that she is…scary. I was going to lie, but you'll find out soon enough, if you haven't already. She is loud and her demands seem unreasonable, but she means well. And, yes, she has an irrational hatred for ranch dressing and mayonnaise, but if you can get beyond all of that she can change your life.

And the best part is that we will no longer have to endure the spectacle Byron makes of himself when he's running on the treadmills. And if we come across him on the trails, there will be plenty of sticks and rocks to pelt him with.

I'm afraid that I am at least partially to blame for the current Byron. While it is true that he came out of the womb shouting, "Let me out of here! I must dance!" I only egged him on. Some would argue that I should have left him how he was: jumping at shadows and trembling at loud noises. There are others that would argue that he would have eventually returned to his old self on his own and that I should have left well enough alone. Perhaps they are right. But you cannot change the past, only endure the consequences of it, and vow to never repeat it.

The experiment I spoke of earlier to rebuild Byron's confidence was a smashing success. The first planned incident was inspired by the near-death experience I had on the bench press. Byron—as he did with nearly every other human endeavor—reveled in the fact that he could lift more weight than everybody else, and I thought this was the best thing to build upon. In the weeks after our confrontation, I had hit the weights more frequently and with much more intensity than ever before, so I was not an uncommon sight on the bench press. I had learned that Byron liked to slip into the weight room shortly after noon, while everyone else was eating lunch. Gone were the days of stripping at the least provocation. Now he wanted to sculpt his body in private, and took to wearing long sleeves and a stocking cap with most of his hair tucked inside.

Some years ago someone gave Kelly a set of fake weight plates as a gag gift. They look, even close up, like the real thing, so if you were to sandwich one of them between actual plates, no one would know the difference. So, with all the glee of someone on the verge of pulling a fast one, I loaded up the bar with two fake 25lb plates on each side and stuck a real one on each end for good measure and waited for Byron to appear. When he did, a few minutes later, I lowered the bar to my chest and proceeded to grunt and writhe. When this failed to get his attention, I called out to him by name and begged him to help me. Sensing a trap, he approached cautiously. But after realizing that I was indeed pinned, he snatched the bar off my chest with ridiculous ease and set it back in the rack. For a moment, his eyes flashed and I knew that the old Byron was still in there somewhere, he just needed a little coaxing. The wheels were turning. He had not only saved the life of his attacker—a very brave and noble thing—but he had also demonstrated that he was by far the stronger of the two of us. This didn't last, however. Once I was off the bench and thanking him profusely, he lowered his eyes, and said weakly, "I'm glad you're all right, Aster."

Over the next several days I made it my mission to build Byron's self-image through whatever means necessary. I paid stranger's grandchildren a dollar a piece to rush up to him and ask to feel his muscles. I spent most of one morning convincing Beverly to invite several of her more attractive friends to lunch so they could make flirty eyes with him and ask to touch his hair. And I made sure that when we crossed paths that I lowered my eyes and scooted towards the opposite wall and tried my best to look petrified.

All of this I did with great joy. I was helping my fellow human being. And how do you suppose I was thanked for all of this? Unbeknownst to me, I had been creating a monster. And monsters, as you know, almost always go for revenge at some point in their careers. So it isn't surprising that one morning while I was sipping my morning coffee, feeling that all was right with the world, he strode up to me with his shirt unbuttoned to mid stomach and his hair newly washed and blow dried and stated that he wanted a rematch. He went on to accuse me of guerrilla tactics and explained that he had been feeling under the weather the day of the attack.

I was torn. Part of me was proud of his return to form and wanted to congratulate him and take him out to celebrate, but another part of me was angered by the way he was turning on his creator.

I still thought myself an aged prize fighter who could step out of retirement at any moment to reclaim the title, so the chance to do battle with this, a confident and worthy opponent, had its attraction. So, without going into too much detail, I accepted the challenge with gusto, feeling just a slight pang at the thought of tearing down what I had spent so much time and effort rebuilding.

Ms. Fisher

Dearest Laverne:

I'm so glad you're coming to the recital. I'm sorry I had to threaten you, but it's been nearly a year since I've seen you in person and I'm starting to forget what you look like. Don't worry about getting your son to drive you. I know he's busy. Randy is trying to make some extra money to get a new guitar, so I'm going to pay him to pick you up. I'm only paying him on your safe arrival, however, which I hope will give him incentive to drive carefully. Make sure you buckle up.

Just when I thought Ernie couldn't get any weirder, he surprises me. I caught him trying to get the nerve up to knock on my door. Now that I know I'm not dying, I've been really ornery, so I snuck up and grabbed his arm and said, "What are you doing!" and he slugged me in the shoulder and ran away. So now when I go get my gallbladder medication, I'll have them look at my bruise. I went to his room later to give him an opportunity to apologize and ask me to the recital, which I assume was what he was going to do before I snuck up on him. He wouldn't answer the door, and he yelled for me to mind my own business. He's coming with us to the recital; he just doesn't know it yet.

Sorry to hit you with this all at once, but I might as well warn you. Unless Art and Jen miraculously work things out in the next two days, Art will be coming with us, too. Don't worry: he's not a vampire. I sprung a cross on him the other evening and he flinched, but only because he thought I was going to hit him with it. I also added seven extra cloves of garlic to the spaghetti sauce last night and it didn't faze him at all.

I told him about the recital, but he doesn't want to go. He's been really depressed and doesn't want to do anything but sleep and watch nature shows. We were watching one the other evening where a gazelle jumped into a lake to try to get away from a lynx that was chasing him, and Art looked at me and said, "I hope he drowns."

He's going to be a delight to have around.

The only way I can get him to shower is if I bribe him with pie or threaten to throw out the remote control. Anyway, I can't leave him alone. I'm afraid he'll get into the nail polish remover. He snuck out the other morning and came back toasty on something. I think he was sniffing gasoline. See what I mean? How can I leave him unattended?

So now people are starting to think that I've got a son nobody knew about, and Beverly told me yesterday that she saw my "man-friend" begging for change out in the parking lot and that he smelled like the "hard stuff." So now I've got a man-friend and a son, both alcoholic drug fiends.

I've decided not to have it out with Jennifer. I forget that this is probably hard on her, too, and since we are incapable of having a conversation without yelling at each other, I figure I'll wait until it blows over. I did leave her a phone message. I tried for chatty and warm, but what came out was, "Your husband is drunk and sleeping on my couch… do something about it. Hope everything is ok." I know I'm hard on her. Art said something cryptic the other day and I can't get it out of my head. The afternoon he was huffing gasoline, he was lying on the floor, and just before he drifted off to sleep he said, "She's a good girl. You should be nicer."

Your only true friend,

B. A. Fisher

From the Archives
The Last Stop Bulletin

The Weather Front

What a bleak morning it is! Even Beverly is affected, which we didn't think was possible. If you are curious what a glum Beverly looks like, peek in the Reception window. If you walk in, she'll flash her winning smile like usual, but if you catch her when she thinks no one is looking, you'll see her chewing her cuticles and tapping her foot nervously. There is something in the air. We've had a creepy feeling all morning. Who cares about the weather when the world is coming to an end…geesh!

Upcoming Events

Up until now, our Events column was full of excitement and anticipation, but ever since SHE got here, there hasn't been anything to get excited about, so we're thinking about renaming the column, Upcoming Atrocities with Helen Watson.

Take a deep breath…The Stamina Stairs we were all so eagerly awaiting are being dismantled as we write this. Helen took one look at them and started gassing up her chainsaw. Harry is eerily calm; Kelly is eerily not. Neither of them was given an opportunity to make a case. Ahem.

We know, we know, we were the ones shouting, "Everything is going to be fine." Not to alarm anyone, but now we're not so sure.

You Ought to Know

There is no need to panic! Our Healthcare staff hasn't been replaced by a swarm of angry bumble bees. We don't mean to make light of your pain. The new uniforms aren't that bad, but we must question the material, which looks like some sort of plastic. The hairnets, to us anyway, seem excessive, and the squeaking of your shiny, plastic shoes, is going to take some getting used to. We'll wrap it up by pointing out that the whiteness of your shoes against the blackness of your "pants" almost makes it look like you're hovering around like little human spaceships... Not to alarm anyone, but an ominous box just showed up for Harry. We hope it's fertilizer or something.

The Suggestion Box

You have spoken and we have listened, but whether or not Helen takes a flying leap off a tall bridge is completely up to her.

The Hot Seat

At this point we feel it unnecessary to use her name. We have decided that it's a waste of ink and trees to keep addressing her and her various offenses. So until someone does something sufficiently heinous to knock you-know-who out of top billing, this column will simply read: See previous nine issues.

P.S. Don't think we've forgotten you, Crocker, we are just changing tactics. We have been in close contact with mafia types who specialize in dealing with people who don't know when enough is enough...sleep with one eye open.

Holy Moses!

Okay, we saved this for the end. It could and probably should have been in the You Ought to Know section, but if we put it there, the rest of the Bulletin would have gone unread...so...we'll wait for you to sit down...and breathe...and breathe...Helen has a cat...Excuse us while we duck for cover.

We have unfortunately confirmed the speculation. She is one of THEM. The little feline's name is Midnight. She is black, duh, and appears soft but we can't confirm it because the little darling won't let us touch her. She has a charming way of luring you in with a couple of sweet murrrrrr's and then screaming and swiping at you like a Samurai Warrior. Considering who raised her, we don't hold it against her. As far as Holy Moses goes, Helen has assured us that they will get along fine, just as long as he respects her space…GOD HELP US.

CASSANDRA

Come in here. I want to show you what I'll be playing...Isn't this thing great? And get this: Mr. Jenson says that when and if they replace it, and when and if he dies, he's going to leave it to me in his will. I told you I'd get a piano somehow. But now I have all sorts of mixed feelings about death and music, which probably isn't healthy. And how I'm going to get it in my apartment god only knows, but I'll deal with that later.

See, it's old, but it's not so bad. And you were all freaked out about it. I don't have to worry about the pedals, either, because Mr. Jenson said that most of the songs we're playing you can get away without using them.

Mr. Jenson's a really good teacher. He's not impatient or anything. Not like the ballet teacher I had when I was a kid that would kick your feet out from under you if you weren't far enough up on your tippy toes. You know what I've been realizing lately? I had a lot of trauma when I was a kid. It's no wonder that I get so worked up about things and expect the worst. I think it's going to be good day and the next thing I know I have paste up my nose, gum in my hair, and I get my feet kicked out from under me.

Before we leave, I want you to go sit way in back, so I can get used to how big this room is. When the screen is down and you're watching a movie, you don't realize it, but when the screen is up and you've got this big stage, and you're up here looking out...Mr. Jenson said that the auditorium will be dark so I won't be able to see anybody beyond the first couple of rows, which will either help or make things worse, I haven't figured out which.

So you want to know the song list? No one else knows, so don't go jabbering around like you normally do...*Endless Love*, as you know. *Crocodile Rock. Lean on Me*, which I'm sure you know. *Werewolves in London*. And we're ending with *Hallelujah*, which you'll understand why at the end. We've got something planned for *Chariots of Fire*, too if I can pull it off, and Mr. Jenson's going to play *In the Summer Time* if his arthritis isn't acting up too much.

So today we were working on *Crocodile Rock* and I was having a hard time with it because of all the stuff you have to do with your left hand. I already told you how my left hand tries to do what my right hand is doing, which makes for some interesting sounds. But it's no big deal now because Mr. Jenson is going to sit next to me and do all the bass parts, which is going to be super fun and take the pressure off me at the same time. We might be able to do that on a few songs.

Endless Love is still going to be the hardest by far because there's a lot going on and I don't want to screw it up, but Mr. Jenson says that he thinks he can figure out a way to simplify the beginning where it will still sound good but won't be so hard, and then I can just play the chords underneath while they're singing.

He has all kinds of tips for me. He said that if I start getting nervous to just remind myself that the audience is just a bunch of old people. He's funnier than I thought he would be. He even suggested that we wear funny hats and sunglasses during *Crocodile Rock* like Elton John used to.

And get this: If we have time and I'm up for it, I'm going to play some of *Moonlight Sonata*. It won't be the whole song; probably just enough to make people cry and throw rose petals...

ASTER

Are you coming to the recital tonight? I have great news on that front: Charlie Bates, whom, as you know, was completely bedbound until recently, is breaking out the slacks and the sport coat and is going to join us. When I see him, I plan on mimicking trumpet noises to signal his triumphant return to life. I have invited Val Kilmeir, too, but he has not confirmed yet, which makes me think that he will be unable to tear himself away from his stamp collection, but I still have hope. Perhaps if I can somehow link tonight's festivities to his favorite pastime I will be able to convince him.

Okay, okay. I can see you screaming at me with your eyes to continue with the Byron affair. I know it was rude to foreshadow such an epic battle and then leave you wondering, so I will continue, but not without hesitation, for the details have sharp edges and cut me still.

There came a point in my training when I started doubting my abilities. Not so much during the daylight hours, but late at night when I was staring at the ceiling. It's hard to lie to yourself when there are no distractions. My training was harder than I imagined. I had told Kelly about the upcoming brawl, and after giving me a long hard look—perhaps trying to figure out if I was pulling her leg, and then trying to decide what atrocities she was going to perform on me if I was—her face lit up and she said, "That's a great idea!" I have struggled with Kelly's enthusiasm. I don't like to think that the reason for her excitement was the thought of me being beaten senseless, but to this day I can't rule it out. As I've stated before, we have had our disagreements. I think there was a part of me that assumed that the news of the fight would spread and the powers that be would intervene and prevent it from happening.

This did not happen. Instead of condemning it, it was treated like Fight Night on HBO, and I was faced with a whole new style of fighting, and in front of a live audience. There would be a ring. There would be rules. There would be gloves and headgear and mouth guards. In a word, there would be boxing, something I finally had to admit I knew nothing about. There would be beer and hotdogs for the spectators and cotton candy for the youngsters. And I have no doubt that if they could have convinced one of the local networks, it would have been televised.

I am a confident man, but I'm smart enough to know when things are stacking up against me. My teeth, which had been so useful in our last fight, were no longer an option. A bell would announce my arrival, so leaping on his back when he wasn't looking was out. Also, we would be doing battle half naked, wearing only boxing trunks, something I'm not accustomed to or comfortable with, whereas Byron would happily spend all of his time in the nude if the laws allowed it. The last aspect of concern was the crowd. The majority of our last fight had taken place in the dark, so I was unable to see those around me. I'm not shy, but nor do I embrace the spotlight like our friend Byron.

I took some comfort in the knowledge that Kelly's Green Giant was going to take time away from uprooting trees with his bare hands to work with me. She also assured me that she knew of a place where I could get a perfectly natural-looking spray-on tan so I wouldn't stand out so much against Byron's bronze, and the red ring ropes. In a rare moment of levity and sarcasm, she suggested that perhaps we should forgo the tan in order to use the glare of my body as another weapon in my arsenal.

The first day of training did nothing to quell my fears. The Green Giant, along with being the size and shape of a small mountain, was an accomplished kick boxer—a terrifying idea—and had a collection of punching bags, which he brought over and set up. The small one— the speed bag, it's called—proved nearly impossible to hit, even when motionless, and the heavy bag—much to my horror—hit back. I suggested that it might help if we painted faces on them to make them more lifelike, which made him laugh but not smile. The first time I hit the heavy bag with a jab that didn't hurt my hand I sprang back and began bouncing around as I imagined Muhammad Ali would. The next thing I knew, the bag crashed into my side and sent me careening across the room as if hit by a wrecking ball. I don't take kindly to inanimate objects throwing their weight around, so I charged back to it and rained a barrage of jabs and elbows down upon it, and when those bounced harmlessly off the bag, I began to shove it until the momentum knocked me off my feet. It was then that the Green Giant suggested we shadow box. I have never felt more nonthreatening in my life.

The final blow came from Kelly. She had been watching my training from afar. She occasionally consulted with The Green Giant, but she hadn't said anything to me directly. As a rule, if Kelly isn't yelling at you it either means that you're doing okay, or you're so far gone that any reaction would be a waste of her time. I was thinking it was the former, but when she finally approached me on my last day of training and put her arm around me and said, "Well, Aster, as long as he doesn't move around you'll be fine. Now let's get you fitted for some thicker headgear," I knew that I was wrong.

The night before the fight was a fitful one. I dreamt of aliens and large dogs wearing boxing gloves, pummeling me—ah, look who it is! Charlie! Over here...I don't mean to be rude, but he's skittish around new people. I will see you later this evening, where we will continue this story hour over by the punch bowl...

Ms. Fisher

Dearest Laverne:

Art's up on the roof. I should have known he'd end up there eventually. He's been up there since early this morning, and he's refusing to come down. I'm trying to decide if I should go out and try to coax him down, or just let things take their course.

He's been on a real destructive streak the last few days. Yesterday morning he was in the shower for forty minutes, so I went in to investigate. You know the last thing in the world I want to see is Art in the shower, but I knew the hot water must have run out a long time before. So when he didn't answer me shouting at him and banging on the door, I had no choice but to barge in.

It was quite the sight. He was lying in the tub trying to drown himself, but the water wouldn't come up over his face because the drain plug doesn't fit snug. He was ghastly white and his teeth were chattering. As you know, I don't suffer fools. "If you want to drown yourself, flip over, you twit," I told him. "Or sit there and die of hypothermia."

The good in me that's been showing up lately made an appearance and made me feel bad, so I threw him a towel and told him that if he wasn't out of the tub in five minutes I was going to come back and throw the hairdryer in with him.

I made him some coffee and went to change my clothes and when I came back he was gone. Out my patio door I noticed a commotion and when I went out I saw that Art was perched on the roof, naked and threatening to jump. So that's where he is. Most of the crowd has left. It would be more interesting if he was more than seven feet off the ground. There's also a nice cushy lilac bush for him to land in, so he'd have to jump half a dozen times and land on his head to boot.

I'm going to have to wrap this up. I just saw Harry dragging the hose around the side of the building, and he didn't look happy. I better stop things before he goes and gets a ladder. If Art forces Harry up on a ladder, he's going to wish he had jumped and landed on his head.

I know all of this is a bit crazy, but don't even think about trying to get out of the recital. I know for a fact that you are in perfect heath, so I will see through any attempts at calling in sick. I'll need all the support I can get. I have left Jen a message about her husband's suicide attempts. Perhaps that will shock her into taking action.

So, anyway, dear, I'm afraid there's going to be all kinds of drama. It will be good for you. You've been sheltered for too long. Welcome to All My Children.

Your only true friend,
B. A. Fisher

From the Archives
The Last Stop Bulletin

The Weather Front

Despite her best efforts Helen has failed to blot out the sun. It will be shining today, but who knows for how much longer.

Upcoming Events

It's been a few hours, so it shouldn't surprise you that Hell-en has initiated some more changes. Hold on to your seats; it's going to be bumpy. It seems that the only thing our Helen is afraid of, besides garlic and holy water, is lawsuits; so much so that she is busy removing every possible threat from our lives, starting with the Fitness Center, which she has deemed a virtual minefield. Apparently she heard of a case in Hoboken where a man's elliptical machine bucked him off and out a second-story window. We think he was probably drunk.

Isn't this fun? We've been reduced to kindergarteners who can't be trusted with adult scissors. Now we can live out our remaining years in safe, sterile silence…Don't give up hope just yet. Kelly was already steaming over the Stamina Stairs, so there's a chance she'll twist Helen into little knots and chuck her in the river…We can only hope.

YOU OUGHT TO KNOW

The "Fireworks" display sucked rocks. We overheard that description being spoken by various grandchildren, and we can't agree more. For those of you not there, we thought You Ought to Know. Really, we've seen more excitement during halftime at little league games. Helen is even more cautious than Harry when it comes to fire safety, which we didn't think was possible. I wonder if she realizes that you can't actually "see" firecrackers and that you can't hear them very well when you're wearing earplugs. Rest assured that no one was more disappointed than Holy Moses, who looked longingly at the real fireworks displays happening on the other side of the river.

The only positive thing we have to report is that Ms. Verney and Katelyn have come to terms with each other. We don't know what went on in the hospital, but they've turned the corner, and Ms. Verney is planning on spending Thanksgiving with Katelyn's family. Unfortunately, they have no idea what they're returning to.

THE HOT SEAT

We are considering discontinuing this column. If someone is capable of dethroning Helen, they ought to be thrown in prison.

THE SUGGESTION BOX

We know.

HOLY MOSES!

Violet and Holy have been getting along like lovers in Vienna, but now Violet is no longer welcome. And if that isn't an example of how black Helen's heart is, we don't know what is. We now can assume that the only reason she is tolerating Holy is because she doesn't want a riot on her hands. She isn't a "dog" person, she tells us. She can't stress this enough. She also isn't a "people" person. We can't stress this enough. We have explained all of this to Holy and he is busy drawing up plans. Brace yourselves.

CASSANDRA

Look at my hands…they're not even shaking. I'm as prepared as I'm going to be so I figure there's no sense worrying about it. Aren't you proud of me? I got a little help, though, I must admit. Mr. Jenson turned me on to these things called beta-blockers that help people with extreme stage fright. I don't know how they work, but I bet you if there was a fire right now, I'd walk over and get some punch. But I don't know if they're legal, so if you see police officers storming the building wave your arms or something.

So have you seen him? Vernon is here. Thank god for the beta-blockers, right? I have all this crazy new strength, but I have my limits. He's over there talking to Beverly. She's so excited. She keeps waving at me and mouthing, "He's here!" and "He's hot!" She also points at him when she thinks he's not looking, which I'm sure doesn't make him uncomfortable at all. I'm just glad I saw him before I go up there and play. Can you imagine if we got to the middle of *Endless Love* and I suddenly spotted him? Then I'd really fall off the piano bench.

These beta-blockers are crazy: when I saw Vernon come in, I walked right up to him and gave him a hug. He's really soft spoken now. So much so that I'm worried about what might have happened to him in prison. It was hard to hear him, but I think he told me that I was going to do great. Apparently beta-blockers do nothing to prevent you from saying something stupid, because I thanked him by saying something brilliant like, "Is Vernon in there?" or "Can I talk to Vernon, please?" I don't even remember which one it was. Does it really matter? Then I suddenly had to pee so I laughed really weird and ran away. So now he's probably trying to figure out how to get back into prison.

Eric's here, too, someplace. Marcus said, "Get out of the kiddy pool!" so I threw Eric in the deep end. I set him up with Minnie, my crazy trainee. I know she's pushy and hyper and she'll totally boss him around but it'll be good for him, and it might slow her down a little bit. Besides, she told me she likes freckles. I don't know if she likes them on guys, or if she just likes them in general, but I figure it's a good sign either way. The last time I saw them she was sitting on his lap over by the buffet table feeding him grapes. They're perfect for each other.

Okay, I guess I better get backstage. We're just about to start. Wish me luck. Oh, I've been trying not to say anything, but do you remember the little demon girl? Well, don't look now, but she's standing right over there and she looks angry…

From the Archives
The Last Stop Bulletin

The Weather Front

The weather will be seasonable warm and dry. Unless it rains. Ha ha.

Upcoming Events

We have decided, with other's input, that the Last Stop Bulletin has been good but has run its course. The information you need will be on the Bulletin board. Thank you for your support over the years. It's been fun.

You Ought to Know

There will be a welcome party for Helen this Friday night. Please bring cookies, juice, and a toy for Midnight.

The Hot Seat

We are in The Hot Seat for wrongly judging Helen and putting hurtful words in the paper. We are ashamed, as we should be.

THE SUGGESTION BOX

You have spoken. There was a suggestion that we put in an outdoor pool. That will not happen. Thank you.

HOLY MOSES!

The dog Holy Moses is being quarantined at the animal shelter for his vicious attack on Helen. We had no idea that he was so aggressive. He might have rabies. That is probably the best place for him. We wish Helen a speedy recovery.

ASTER

There you are! I have been looking all over. Not really, but I thought I'd make you feel good. Don't look so glum; I knew I would run into you sooner or later. I must warn you that the punch is not punch. Someone has gone out of his way to give it some kick. I'm not naming any names.

So we must be quick. I have sent Charlie for triangle sandwiches and fruit cups. The sandwiches he will find, but he will be searching high and low for the fruit cups because there aren't any. He has been physically and mentally inactive for so long that these brain teasers will be good for him. I have been doing these sorts of things to him since he got here. He will realize before too long that I have tricked him again, and he will return with an apologetic smile, which will quickly turn to a horrified grimace when he sees us talking and realizes that he has to join a conversation already in progress. So, I repeat: we must be quick!

Round One:

I come out bouncing around, trying to make myself a moving target, and proceed to trip over my shoelace—no doubt untied by some Bryon supporter as I was climbing into the ring—and begin sprinting across the ring to try to stop myself from falling on my face. My arms are flailing, and I'm pretty sure I'm yelling as I go, but I don't remember. Byron smiles as he sidesteps to let me go by, whereupon he turns and punches me in the back of the head. This, I am to understand, is payback for latching onto his ear in our last fight. I fall to the mat and consider staying there for all eternity until the crowd begins to boo and the grandchildren begin pelting me with lemon drops. I get back to my feet after an absurdly slow eight count, whereupon I try to collect myself, but Byron is charging. My training at this point is completely forgotten and I remember thinking how disappointed the Green Giant must be. I make one feeble attempt at bringing my hands up before being hit by two left jabs and then being hammered with a right hook that sends me sprawling. The force of the blow spins my headgear around so that the back portion is now in front and covering one eye. I begin to panic because the other eye is watering profusely and I am unable to see. I army-crawl across the ring, pull myself up using the ropes and then begin running in small circles. Oh, how the children laughed! And then comes the final death blow. Byron, unbeknownst to me, has been tracking me all around the ring, waiting for the perfect opening, which he finds when I raise my hands to fix my crooked headgear. He unleashes an uppercut to my midsection that first doubles me over and then causes me to fall head first to the mat. I land and perfectly balance on the crown of my head in a manner any ostrich would be proud of and wait out the ten count.

I didn't see it, but I am told that Byron ran circles around the ring, yelling, "Number One!" and throwing his head around. I take some comfort in the fact that the crowd did not take part in the celebration, and I am proud of the next generation for turning their lemon drops on him—

Hello, Charlie! I see that you come offering triangle sandwiches…No, no, don't run, don't run! I have no idea who this person is…

Well, I guess we were quick but not quick enough. This calls for more punch and triangle sandwiches. I leave you to the task. Bring enough for Ruby, too. Before she had time to think about it, she agreed to join us this evening. She says she still finds me charming from a distance.

FROM THE ARCHIVES
DESTROY AFTER READING

We shouldn't have to tell you that we were not the authors of that humorless, apologetic, semi-literate bile that was masquerading as a Last Stop Bulletin. SHE hijacked our computer when we weren't looking. So now it's confirmed. She is the devil. If she wants to play dirty, so be it. From this moment forward, The Last Stop Bulletin is officially underground. We will not sit idle while Helen destroys everything Mary Stuart stands for. Will you? This is a call to arms. Rise up! Show no mercy!

The Last Stop Bulletin will hereby be delivered to your rooms under the cover of darkness. Absolute secrecy is vital to the success of our mission. Be strong and we will conquer. In the words of Sun Tzu:

"Fein disorder, and crush her!"

Ms. Fisher

Shield me for a minute, won't you? I need a break from my company. Is my nose bleeding? It feels like its bleeding. He wacked me pretty good.

I don't think we've met. I've seen you around. Let me give you a piece of advice. You see Ernie over there? The one looking as though he expects a saber-toothed tiger to spring out from underneath one of the tables? Whatever you do, don't startle him. He reacts with violence. I grabbed his arm so we could go dance and he elbowed me in the nose. He's my date and he doesn't like to be touched. Isn't that nice? I've already got a bruise the size of an apple on my shoulder. Not one of his more charming characteristics.

There's a rumor going around that the punch is spiked. I can only hope—and now they've spotted me. I was hoping they could entertain themselves for a while, but I guess I am the life of the party.

So...the little one there, the one with the puffy eyes, that's Art, my son-in-law, and he has been crying off and on since early this morning. Don't ask. The one walking behind him doing her best to look miserable is my daughter, Jennifer. Doesn't she look happy? Like a ray of sunshine. She doesn't like old people. Can you imagine not liking old people? What's not to like? And then, off to the side there, that's Ernie, of course. He doesn't like anyone behind him...or in front of him...or around him in general. I won't bother introducing him when he gets here. He won't be in hearing range. And that one there, dancing, is my saving grace, Laverne, who is here on vacation to save me from the other three.

You know I had hoped that I might be able to change little Ernie, but it's like trying to perform surgery from down in the parking lot. I still might give it a shot. He called me ravishing once and nobody calls me ravishing and gets away with it.

What did you say your name was?

The Excommunication of Helen Performed by The Last Stop Theater Group

Special appearance by Holy Moses

Scene 1

Setting: Lobby.

Beverly is in the middle of an important conversation. Helen (played by Ms. Langley) stands by, impatiently tapping her foot and glaring down at her with obvious venom. She looks on the verge of attack. After a moment, she snatches the receiver out of Beverly's hand and slams it on the counter. She then orders Beverly to clean up her work area (improvisation). Helen is about to turn and leave when Holy Moses comes bounding in. He has obviously been rolling around in some unknown substance. His feet are muddy, and he has recently been drinking so strings of drool hang from his jowls. Helen glares at him in disbelief. Holy Moses, sensing a murderous rampage, shakes his head vigorously, showering everything around him, including Helen, and runs away. Helen gives chase. A commotion is heard off stage (shouting, things crashing, etc.) ending with a growl from Holy and a scream from Helen.

SCENE 2

Setting: Helen's suite.

Helen is sleeping peacefully. We can see that part of her arm is bandaged, as well as her left foot. We notice the exterior door being opened. Ms. Crocker enters, crouched down and moving slowly towards the bed. She is leaving a trail of nuts and bread and raisins behind her. A succession of animals large and small begins to file in. First, a raccoon (played by child 1), then a small otter (played by child 2), then two mule deer (played by Mandy M and Sandy D) followed by three skunks (played by child 3, 4, and 5) Taking up the rear is a small, malnourished moose (played by Mr. Richardson.) The raccoon and otter flank the bed to the right, while the skunks position themselves on the left. Ms. Crocker, motioning to the deer and moose, points to the raisin that she has just placed on Helen's nose. The deer and moose move in excitedly and Helen wakes to find them both staring down at her. Helen screams. She stands up in bed. She jumps up and down. She faints, falls back and rolls off the right side of the bed. The animals rejoice.

SCENE 3

Setting: Hallway.

Helen enters from stage right, her hand bandaged, her left arm in a sling, a patch over one eye. She is dragging her leg behind her. You almost feel sorry for her until, with her good hand, she produces a white cloth and runs it across the door jam and then looks at the dust disapprovingly. She hasn't noticed the coordinated mob slowing coming up behind her. Mr. Ukley, looking like a deranged madman, is holding a rope. Ms. Carlisle is behind him, grinning devilishly and holding duct tape. Helen turns just as Mr. Ukley tackles her. She has no time to scream.

SCENE 4

Setting: Unknown storage room.

Helen is bound to a chair, her mouth covered in tape and her arms and legs tied. Midnight, her beloved cat, is in a carrier in front of her. Mr.

Ukley picks up the carrier so she can see the black animal inside. Helen begins cursing (under her breath, please, there are children). Mr. Ukley begins to laugh and shake the carrier violently. From around the corner, we see Donna push play on a tape machine that begins the *When Cat's Attack* soundtrack. The tape covering Helen's mouth has worked itself off and she begins yelling and straining against the ropes. "Stop it! Stop it!" she screams, or something similar.

Scene 5

Setting: The lobby.

A group is gathered and is talking excitedly amongst themselves. A door is heard opening and Helen enters, dragging a suitcase behind her. Midnight is on a leash but is walking by herself. As she picks her way through the crowd, Holy Moses, wearing a striped jail jacket, steps behind Beverly for protection. Helen stops and turns as if to address the crowd, then lowers her head and continues her march off stage left. The house band breaks into an upbeat version of *Hallelujah*. The crowd sings along.

Disclaimer: Details have been altered slightly, and some scenes omitted to protect all those involved. This is for entertainment purposes only, and is not an accurate representation of actual events.

• Donations are still being accepted to cover legal expenses for the upcoming trial.

THE NEW LAST STOP BULLETIN

THE WEATHER FRONT

Someone once said of Colorado weather, "If you don't like the weather, wait a minute." We were all prepared to write a glowing description of the sunshine and the bird chatter, but now that we glance out the window, dark clouds have sprung up and the birds are diving for cover. So if you want to know what the weather's going to be like, wait a minute.

YOU OUGHT TO KNOW

The recital was a success! Here are some of the highlights:

First, Cassandra did a bang up job filling in for Mr. Jenson, and Mr. Jenson did a bang up job limiting himself to the lower half of the piano. The songs were both moving and funny and the outfits gave us fits. *Moonlight Sonata* as an encore was…we never even saw the tears coming. Good Job! We can't wait to see what you come up with for Christmas.

Holy's performance in *The Excommunication of Helen* was spot on, but why would we expect anything less? We only wish we could have worked Violet into the skit somehow. We'll work on that for next year. We would like to thank the children who played the various animal parts. We applaud you for your focus, even when Helen (Ms. Langley) began sneezing.

Nathan's Lasagna was wonderful. Congratulations to him on his first Entrée. Don't listen to the rumor going around that the sauce was thin. We'd like to see them do better with an angry French chef with a penchant for throwing things looking over their shoulder. Besides, it was your first time: you were bound to be nervous.

Now for a couple of highlights that may have gone unnoticed to the untrained eye. Katelyn went back five times for lasagna but only actually came back with lasagna twice. We're thinking that maybe she was more interested in the cook than she was in the lasagna. Call us crazy. And some of you were skeptical. You know what this means? We're thinking Jesse would be a good name for their first born.

Chariots of Fire was a fine way to end the evening. After Cassandra reduced us to blubbering fools, Byron had us buckled over when he performed his Olympic routine and stripped down to reveal—for those of you who forgot your glasses—another shirt that read, "Don't look at me, I'm naked!"

Some of you have expressed interest in performing in next year's *The Excommunication of Helen*, so rest assured that we are coming up with additional parts. Some of you may have to be lamps and furniture, but we'll get as many of you involved as possible. Not everyone can perform in it, however, because then who would be left to enjoy it?

Upcoming Events

THE STAMINA STAIRS ARE FINALLY FINISHED AND WILL OPEN TOMORROW SO YOU CAN STOP ASKING US ABOUT THEM FOR GODS SAKE! No, we didn't anticipate it taking this long to complete, but once you see the final product you will appreciate the time and effort Harry put into them. And just so everyone knows, they are indestructible. Somehow Harry has managed to tie them into the foundation of the building, so in order to get rid of them you'd have to knock down the whole facility. There is going to be a lottery drawing to pick who goes first, so see Beverly for your ticket.

Now, we don't want to alarm any of you—or excite you, as the case may be—unnecessarily, but there is talk that the land to the southeast is going to be developed into a golf course. Now, before you start jumping for joy or printing out petitions, we must say it again: It is only talk. We just thought you should be prepared.

This should probably go in The Hot Seat but we are lacking the courage to put him there. Several people—who have since been entered into the witness protection program—spotted Harry dumping the contents of an unmarked bottle into the punch bowl. While we don't encourage drugging people without their knowing it, we must ultimately thank him for the loose mood it created. However, there were children in attendance, so we are being careful not to go too far in our praise. As far as we know, the children stuck to the juice boxes and soda.

THE HOT SEAT

We must state up front that this isn't really deserving of The Hot Seat, but there were tears involved, so we feel we have no choice. Ms. Langley, your performance as Helen in *The Excommunication of Helen* was Oscar-worthy—so much so that it was a bit disarming. Somehow you managed to channel Helen through you, which must have been even scarier than it looked. So, what might seem an odd request, we must insist that you tone it down next year. We don't have to tell you that Beverly was reduced to tears when you started yelling at her in Scene 1. And some of us—particularly those with grandchildren in the seats next to them—found your choice of words during the offstage fight with Holy Moses a bit too colorful.

Now for our real Hot Seat recipient: Walter, Walter, Walter, alcohol is not food. We looked it up. What you do in the privacy of your room is your business, but when you take your wine out to the porch and sing songs at seven in the morning, we feel we must step in. Besides, you are infringing on Robert's territory. We are not a halfway house. We hate to do this in public, but since you've barricaded yourself in your room, you leave us no choice. You are going to get an intervention whether you like it or not. So continue if you must, but we must tell you that Kelly has been informed of your recent binge drinking and has summoned The Green Giant, who will gladly knock your door down if need be.

THE SUGGESTION BOX

Let us, as the writers and producers of *The Excommunication of Helen*, apologize right up front. We are sorry for any psychological trauma we may have caused. We received no fewer than fifty-three suggestions that we don't "abuse helpless animals by shaking them in carriers." We're sorry. We thought it was obvious that there wasn't an actual cat in the carrier, but we realize it was dark. We have spoken to Mr. Ukley about not shaking the carrier quite so violently in future performances, and we're toying around with the idea of taking the stuffed animal out of the carrier at the end and throwing it into the audience so there will be no doubt. Also, if there is anyone left who doesn't know, as much as Midnight disliked all of us, the feeling was never mutual. Midnight's role in the actual *Excommunication of Helen* was that of the helpless bystander.

HOLY MOSES!

Holy Moses is a star. Just when we thought his celebrity status had reached its peak, he goes and gives the performance of a lifetime: the way he positioned himself as to remain in the scene without blocking the audience's view, and the way he shook himself so that most of the drool ended up on Helen was both considerate and appropriate. The chase scene will be studied by animal trainers for years. The tail tucked; the ears pinned back; the butt hovering just slightly over the flooring, giving the appearance of flight was the work of a great stage actor. Who knew he was taking acting lessons? We saw him earlier, and he was busy working on his acceptance speech.

P.S. If anyone knows who the little man trying to sell his stamps during the recital was, please let us know so we can ban him from further events.

Made in the USA
Monee, IL
21 December 2019

19291445R00108